Down for the Count

Count

a Dare Me novel

Christine Bell

Entangled Publishing, LLC
2614 South Timberline Road
Suite 109
Fort Collins, CO 80525
Visit our website at www.entangledpublishing.com.

Brazen is an imprint of Entangled Publishing, LLC. For more information on our titles, visit www.brazenbooks.com.

Edited by Heather Howland and Kerri-Leigh Grady
Cover design by Heather Howland

ISBN   978-1-62266-822-9

Manufactured in the United States of America

First Edition September 2012

The author acknowledges the copyrighted or trademarked status and trademark owners of the following wordmarks mentioned in this work of fiction: "Twist and Shout," "Mony Mony," Harley, Mustang, Irish Spring, Airsoft, Powerpuff Girls, Jack Daniel's, "Kumbaya," Sharpie, Guinness World Records, Coke, Twinkie, Olympics, Civic, Dom Pérignon, The Weather Channel, *Dirty Dancing*, "Will You Still Love Me Tomorrow," "Rockin' Robin," "The Stroll," Spice Girls, "Two Princes," Spin Doctors, Heart, *Good Will Hunting*, Chanel, Bentley, *Dr. Phil*, El San Juan Resort, ESPN, *Men in Black, Blue Lagoon*.

For my husband, Chip. Thanks for the boxing lessons, babe. Another love TKO.

Chapter One

Lacey Garrity—soon to be Clemson once she got down to the social security office to change it— marched up the long corridor between the reception hall and the bar, muttering to herself. It was time to throw the frigging bouquet, but her groom was MIA. After making a list of possible places he might have gone, jotted neatly on a cocktail napkin, she'd made the rounds and so far? *Nada*.

Pausing, she jabbed at the green call button of her cell phone and held it to her ear.

In the reception room behind her, the strains of "Twist and Shout" faded. It was only that brief absence of music that allowed her to hear the muffled, familiar melody of Marty's ringtone coming from behind a door at the end of the hallway. *Bah dum. Bah dum. Bahdum bahdum bahdum…*

Relief flooded her, and she beelined toward the sound. She tugged the door open and—

"Marty?" Lacey stared down at her husband of two hours, total shock momentarily preventing her from comprehending the scene before her. The slightly muffled version of *The Pink Panther* theme song coming from the pants around her husband's ankles kept time with the *ring* pouring from the receiver of the telephone she still had cupped to her ear.

"Lacey! I can explain," Marty said as he frantically tried to extract himself from the woman he was screwing and yank up his pants at the same time, which was no easy feat given the restrictive confines of the filled-to-bursting storage closet. In his struggle, he knocked a mound of snowy-white linens off the shelf behind him, and they toppled onto his paramour with a *thunk,* shoving her torso flat into the table she was draped over.

"Shit!" she wailed, floundering until the cloths fell to the floor in a heap.

Lacey focused more intently on the woman ass up in front of Marty. Black curls arranged in an updo, a tasteful navy dress bunched around her bare thighs. Navy chiffon, to be exact. The very same chiffon she'd picked out for her bridesmaid dresses.

Shock gave way to a gut-wrenching sense of betrayal. "Becca?" Her brain thrashed around in search of a stronghold, a port in this most ludicrous of storms, and she uttered the first thing that came to mind. "But you said he had woman-hips."

"Hi, this is Marty. Leave a message," the oh-so-familiar voice chirped in her ear.

"Hi, Marty?" she said into the previously forgotten phone. "This is Lacey. You're a lying piece of shit asshole." She disconnected and hurled it against the corridor wall, where it connected with a satisfying *crunch*.

Marty flinched. "Honey, it's not what it looks like."

Why do people always say that? she wondered dully.

Becca tugged at the hem of her dress and stared at the floor, slump-shouldered and unwilling to meet Lacey's gaze.

"What it looks like is that you're having sex with one of my oldest friends in the linen closet of our reception hall.

Unless, of course, she's lost something in her vagina and you were gallant enough to try and fish it out for her. With your penis. If that's the case, I suggest using a larger lure."

A whispered "Ouch" over her shoulder clued her in to the fact that the three of them were no longer alone. Her skin prickled like she'd been dipped in rubbing alcohol, but she kept her gaze locked on Marty.

He winced, his cheeks turning a fiery shade of red. "No need to be rude, Lace." The ensuing silence was so absolute that when he fastened his tuxedo pants, it sounded like a grizzly bear traveling down a zip line.

"Please tell me you're not chastising me over my lack of manners right now. Because if I thought that were true, I just might get one of those stupid shrimp forks your mother insisted we have and jam it into your eye."

He gaped at her as if he'd never seen her before and wasn't all that thrilled with the view. Well, bully for him. She knew the feeling.

"Lacey, we were going to tell you. But things got out of hand, and then the merger…" Becca's blue eyes pleaded with her. For what? Understanding? Forgiveness?

She was fresh out of both.

Tears pricked the backs of her lids, and she stared at two of the people she thought she could count on most. Lifting her trembling hand, she tore off her wedding and engagement rings, then set the now meaningless symbols of commitment carefully on the table.

"That's it?" an outraged voice bellowed from over her shoulder. "You're going to let them off that easy? Oh, no way. Not on my watch." Her maid of honor and sister from another mister, Cat Thomas, pushed past her and peered in. Her green eyes were a bit bleary as she treated the couple in the closet to a death stare. "I should kick your prissy little ass."

She was probably talking to Becca, but it was a fitting threat for both of them, and that made the whole thing even more awful. Marty wouldn't have even *considered* bending Lacey over a table, never mind one in the linen closet of a public place, but there he'd been, doing exactly that with her friend. On their wedding day.

"Cat, stay out of it," a low male voice murmured.

Lacey closed her eyes and bit back a groan. Of all the people to have witnessed her shame, Galen Thomas would've been her last choice. Cat's brother had been away for the past eight months training for a fight, and he'd just returned to Rhode Island. Lacey had been so sure he would still be at home recovering, she'd never expected him to come to the wedding.

Growing up, he had been a never-ending source of torment for Lacey, either unaware or unimpressed with the fact that she'd harbored a serious crush on him since grade school. In spite of his ribbing and her efforts to act like she couldn't care less, over the years they'd forged an uneasy alliance for Cat's sake. She hated him seeing her at her lowest point. Especially after he'd warned her about Marty the year before.

His muttered, "Watch yourself, squirt. He's spineless, and spineless people don't care who gets hurt, so long as it's not them," had stuck with her far longer than it should have.

Or maybe not long enough, she thought glumly and took one last look at the train wreck in front of her.

"I'm fine, Cat. Galen's right. I need to go before any of the other guests see this." She met Marty's miserable gaze. "You'll be hearing from my lawyer. Don't try to contact me. I have nothing to say to you."

She turned to Becca and the ache in her gut increased tenfold. For a brief moment, she wondered if it should be the other way around. Shouldn't *his* betrayal hurt worse? But before she could catch hold of the thought, it burned away under the heat of white-hot anger at Becca. The third amigo. The *other* sidekick for the force that was Cat. The person she could call when she just wanted to vent instead of plot to take over the world. If Cat was the meat of their sandwich, Lacey and Becca were the slices of bread.

Not anymore.

Sweet, sweet Becca was now Becca the Betrayer.

"And you?" She cast around for something to say, to lash out, to make her pay, but all she could muster was, "I want my 'N-Sync T-shirt back. Then lose my number."

Becca's mouth opened and closed soundlessly, her pink cheeks going chalk white.

The tears were coming soon. They were building at the back of her throat like an imprisoned scream. She had to get out of there, fast. Cat took her arm and led her across the hall with a hissed, "Bastards," over her shoulder. Galen fell into step on her other side.

"Is this a nightmare? Please tell me this is a nightmare," Lacey murmured under her breath.

"This is no nightmare, squirt. This is the luckiest day of your life," Galen said, his tone grim.

"*Not* the time, bro." Cat popped her brother hard on the shoulder with a balled-up fist.

"It's the truth. That guy wasn't good enough to wipe your shoes. And your friend there is getting exactly what she deserves. A jellyfish of a man for a jellyfish of a woman. She always was weak."

There was an uncharacteristic compliment buried in that statement, and it registered briefly through her shock, but she didn't have a chance to dwell on it. They'd reached the main reception hall filled with her family and friends. The black cloud of dread hanging over her thickened. The wedding was supposed to have paved the way for two of the city's most high-powered law firms to merge into one big family firm. Now that might never happen and, despite the circumstances being out of Lacey's control, her mother was going to be furious.

She paused and ran a hand over her hair, the strains of "Mony Mony" pouring through the doors increasing her agitation tenfold. "I have to go in there, don't I? To tell them something?" Her voice warbled and she bit her lip.

"Nope. Galen will tell them. I'll drive you to your apartment to change your clothes, and we'll go get smashed!" Cat held up a hand for a high five.

"Not going to happen," Galen cut in. "You're already smashed," he said to his sister before turning to Lacey. "And you're in no condition to drive. You're still in shock, and when this hits the fan, it's going to get ugly."

He was right. Cat had been sipping mimosas all morning and had drunk more than her share at cocktail hour. Her flaming-red hair had escaped its confines and the makeup that had been flawless—if liberally applied—earlier in the day was now smudgy around her bleary green eyes. It would be wrong to let her get behind the wheel. Lacey had enjoyed a couple herself, but clearly not enough to dull this pain. Galen had hit the nail on the head. She was one false move from shattering into a million pieces.

Run away, her mind screamed. For once, she went with impulse over common sense.

"Cat, go tell Marty *he* can let the guests know why I've left. He's a big, fat, stupid liar, so I'm sure he'll come up with a plausible reason. But tell him if he makes it look like it was my fault, he'll regret it. And make sure he tells them to take their gifts home. Oh, and try to manage my mother, okay? I hate to put you in that spot, but she is going to flip out and I can't handle her brand of crazy right now when I haven't even had a chance to have my own."

"No problem. Leave The Admiral to me."

Cat's nickname for her mother usually brought a smile to Lacey's face, but not today. Today, she winced at the accuracy of the name. Things hadn't gone The Admiral's way, and she wasn't going to be happy with her little sailors. The question was, would she try to be understanding or would she blame it on Lacey—again?

"I owe you huge for this. I just need some time before I can face the fallout." She turned to pin Galen with a frank stare, ready to beg if she needed to. But when she faced him fully for the first time, her heart hitched. His dark hair was tousled, and his chin bore the scruff that was ever-present unless he was prepping for a fight. True to form, he was underdressed in a sports jacket that stretched tight over his wide shoulders and jeans that had seen better days. She'd spent thousands of her waking hours picturing that face, and just as many sleeping hours dreaming of it. A pang of regret for what never was joined the other riot of emotions from this hellacious day, and when she met his brown eyes, the pity there was more than she could bear. The tears flowed freely and she swallowed the last morsel of her pride. "Can you get me the hell out of here, please?"

• • •

For a long moment, Galen held her amber gaze and didn't respond, although his instincts were bleating up a storm. *This is a baaaaad idea.* His instincts were pretty fucking solid most days and had saved him a lot of pain, both in the ring and out. In fact, hadn't he told Lacey not to marry this loser? He opened his mouth to remind her of that fact again but snapped it shut a second later when his instincts told him a move like that would earn him a high-heeled kick to the family jewels. "And go where?"

"Anywhere, blockhead," Cat cut in with a roll of her eyes. "She has to get out of here. You two go. I'll deal with everything here."

Lacey gave her a weak smile. "Thanks, Cat. I'd be lost without you."

"Tell me about it. And don't worry. If Loverboy tries to throw you under the bus, I'll make sure everyone hears the truth," she assured Lacey, giving her arm a gentle pat.

Galen *really* didn't want to get involved in this mess. Something had been happening over the past couple years, and he didn't like it. The obligatory annoyance combined with grudging affection that guys typically felt toward the good longtime friends of their sisters had begun to change when it came to Lacey. She was no longer a gangly, awkward teen—and he knew it. Luckily, that was right about the time she'd saddled herself with Marty the dishrag, so it hadn't been an issue. Hell, he'd only come because his sister's latest boy toy had bailed, and she needed a plus one. "Listen, I—"

"Galen. Please. I can't go back in there." Lacey's voice had lost the shrill gloss of panic and now sounded resigned. Beat down.

God, he was a sucker. He closed his eyes for a long moment and nodded. "Okay. I've got my bike, though." He cast a dubious eye at her floor-length gown.

"We'll make it work." With the promise of imminent escape, she sounded stronger already. She jammed her arm through his so their elbows were locked and raised her chin. "Cat, I'll call you later once I'm settled."

"You threw your phone," Galen reminded her.

"Indeed I did." Her chin dipped a little before she rebounded like a champ. "Cat, I will *e-mail* you later if I can't find a phone."

"Cool. Love you, babe. And I promise, in a few months, after we've exacted our revenge, we're going to look back at this and laugh," Cat said.

Galen frowned and his sister shrugged. Between the two of them, they were screwing this up royally. Maybe he'd think of something good to say on the way out.

He led Lacey toward the main exit, but she tugged him toward the bar in the deserted lounge area. "One second." She yanked her arm from his. "Excuse me, sir?" she called to the balding bartender washing glasses at an industrial-sized sink in the corner. Balancing precariously on the wooden footrest skirting the bar, she reached over the counter and plucked a bottle of champagne nestled in an ice bin. "Put this on my husband's tab, would you? Marty Clemson, the wedding in the Rose Room."

She didn't wait for a response but stalked out the door with the bottle clutched in her hand.

He stared helplessly after her, then looked back to the bartender. "Can you even do that?"

The guy shrugged. "What am I going to do, chase after her? Given the look on her face, I'm going to say that seems like a bad idea."

Galen sighed, reached into his pocket, and pulled out a fifty. "Will that cover it?"

"Yep."

Two seconds later, he exited the building and glanced around. Lacey had stopped at his Harley and set down the champagne. She couldn't ride with that gown on. She'd get them both killed. They were going to have to—

He paused mid-step when Lacey reached behind her

neck. What was she going to do, strip?

"Some help here?" she mumbled, grappling with the hooks down her back.

Some help here? Little Lacey Garrity wanted his help taking off her wedding dress. The shy teen his sister had forced to drink four wine coolers before she would go skinny-dipping. And even then, she'd made them all close their eyes until she was in up to her neck. This was officially the weirdest fucking day of his life. "I'm not sure exactly what the plan is, but I can tell you right now, it's ill-advised," he said, ignoring the baser part of him that roared to life at the thought of seeing what was under all that dress.

"Damn it," Lacey muttered, scrabbling at the catches.

He didn't dare smile. She might not be gangly anymore, but she was still a little awkward, in the way that a woman was when she had no true sense of her worth. But that aside, the outer packaging was right and tight. Easy enough to put it out of his mind when she was engaged to another man. Not so easy now that her relationship had disintegrated and she wanted him to help her disrobe.

"I'll help you if you tell me what we're hoping to accomplish. You can't ride on the back of my bike naked. You realize that, right?"

"I have a full slip under here that comes down to my knees. It's no more revealing than some cocktail dresses I've seen, so don't worry. I won't get us arrested."

The emotionless resignation in her tone made him want to go back into the hall and treat Marty Clemson to the uppercut that had earned him the nickname Whalin' Galen. One shot, right to the fucker's nonexistent chin. But then he saw the tremble. It wasn't much, just a little shiver of uncertainty that snaked through her and left her readable. And what he read spelled sadness. The deep, *I don't even know what to do with myself* kind of pain. Damn.

At that moment, if she'd asked him to dance a jig, he'd have considered it if it meant cheering her up even a little. He stalked up behind her to push her hands out of the way. "I'll do it. We're going to have to take it really slow riding. If we took a spill, your legs would be a mess."

The slender line of neck teased him, and he vowed to make quick work of it. He'd gotten through the first trillion buttons and was about halfway done when her shoulders started to shake.

He froze. "Are you crying?"

"Can you hurry?" She loosed a pathetic sniffle. "I just want to go."

He eyed the long line of pearls dubiously. Making an executive decision, he grasped both sides in his hands and yanked. The dress split in two down to the middle of her thighs. He let it drop into a pool at her feet and she didn't even blink when she stepped out of it.

"Thanks," she said with a brave, watery smile.

He nodded but opted not to speak. She was right. The slip did cover her, much in the way a coat of candy-apple-red paint covered a Mustang. It didn't so much hide the car as it enhanced exactly how badass it was. Spaghetti straps of white silk lay in stark relief against the darker, golden skin of her shoulders. Her full breasts strained at the material binding them. If he looked a little harder he'd just be able to make out the contour of her nipples —

"Why are you staring at me like that?" Her sad eyes went wide. "Is there a bug on me? Is it a spider?" She screeched the last word and began frantically swiping at her slip.

"No, you're fine. Stop it. I was thinking what a douche bag Marty is." It was as close to the truth as he could manage, given the circumstances.

She stopped all her fussing and stared at him. "Thanks. I appreciate that. Now get me out of here before people start coming out, would you?"

"Where to, squirt?"

"Not home."

He waited for further instructions, but that was clearly all he was getting out of her. "Not home it is." He yanked his helmet off the handlebar and plunked it on her head. "Tighten the chin strap."

He took the bottle from her and stowed it in his pack, then climbed on. When she straddled the seat behind him, he had to steel himself. Her slip rode up high enough to reveal slim, toned legs encased in silk stockings. A thin, lace garter in blue and white hugged one thigh. She snuggled in close, molding her front to his back, and he said a silent little prayer.

Dear Satan. I don't know why you're testing me, but I don't like it. No love, Galen.

Chapter Two

Lacey shuddered, pressing her face against the warmth of Galen's broad back. What had started off as a balmy afternoon had turned into a crisp evening. She seriously regretted stripping off her dress and regretted leaving it in the parking lot even more.

Not just a dress, she reminded herself. Her wedding gown. With its delicate row of seed-pearl buttons meant for the eager fingers of a man who loved her more than anything else in the world. Instead, it had been torn off by a guy who couldn't give two craps about her, aside from some ingrained but reluctant sense of responsibility. She sniffled and shoved the thought away. Marty wasn't worthy of that dress anyway.

"Are we almost there?" she shouted, suppressing another shiver. Galen had offered his jacket more than once, but she'd put him out enough for one day.

He nodded. She wrapped her arms tighter around his middle and closed her eyes, breathing in the comforting smell of Irish Spring soap that had been the Thomas family's preference for as long as she'd known them. She tried not to think about the past few hours or the difficult days to come, but she was a planner down to her very marrow and the latter went against the grain. Fact was, she had no clue what the hell she was going to do now. All her neatly laid-out plans had been soundly obliterated with one bang. Literally.

Actually, that might be putting too much of a shine on it. It could've been multiple bangs. With multiple women. She thought she'd known Marty better than that, but now? Blech. Anything was possible. Thank God on the rare occasions they'd actually done anything in bed, she'd insisted he use a condom despite his complaints. And to think, tonight was the night she'd planned to tell him she'd gone on the Pill in hopes of ramping up their love life. She'd thought her wedding night would be the night she finally got to see what all the fuss was about. And now this.

Bastard.

In an effort to keep the anger burning hot enough to distract her from the sting of her wounded pride, fear of the unknown, and depressing thoughts about Becca, she spent the remainder of the ride concocting wild revenge schemes, most of which involved red ants, honey, and Marty's testicles. She'd finally settled on a winner when the deafening rumble of the bike stopped abruptly.

She opened her eyes and saw the Thomas family's lake cottage. The saltbox house was painted a faded china blue and had been for as long as she could remember. She'd loved this place growing up, and the memories of long summer days filled with ice-cream sandwiches and catching fireflies wrapped around her wounded soul like a quilt. Grateful tears clogged her throat, and she bit her lip.

"This is our stop. Okay for you?" Galen said, and flipped out the kickstand with the heel of his boot. "We can at least get you some clothes and a glass of that bubbly until you figure out where to go next."

"Perfect." She slipped off the bike and stretched, surprised at the stiffness in her thighs. She must have been holding on more tightly than she realized. Tugging off the helmet, she met Galen's gaze.

Their relationship over the years had been mostly snide banter with the occasional big-brother warning mixed in, but he'd gone above and beyond today and it was imperative he knew how much she appreciated it. On a day like this one, that kind of loyalty meant something. She hadn't just lost her husband. She'd lost one of her closest friends. Cat and Galen coming through for her was one of the few things she had to cling to.

"You're a saint for rescuing me. I can't thank you enough." She bent and pressed a kiss to his cheek, then turned to jog up the stairs before he could react.

She knew from experience what had happened today was all going to somehow come down on her. Her mother was the queen of assigning blame. Lacey made a decision in that second. She wasn't talking to any of them about the merger or anything else until she had some time to lick her wounds and repair her armor. It was going to get ugly, and the accusations would fly, mostly in her direction. "Not your fault, Lace," she muttered.

"Most definitely not," Galen agreed. He climbed onto the porch and gave her shoulder an awkward rub. "I don't care how annoying you are; no one deserves that."

She gaped at him for a second before catching the mirth in his eyes in the moonlight. Taking comfort in the familiar, she snorted. "Me, annoying? This from the guy who used to let the air out of my bike tires on a regular basis."

He bent his head, squinted at the lock, and slipped in the key. "I only did that when you guys would use my Airsoft guns to play Powerpuff Girls."

The laugh that escaped was genuine. "How did you know it was me? Maybe it was Cat."

"Seriously? You labeled them 'Blossom,' 'Bubbles,' and 'Buttercup.' With a label maker."

The door swung open and she followed him in, smiling at the memory. She'd loved that label maker. "You know your sister. If I didn't label everything, we'd fight and she'd take the good one every time and swear it was hers."

"You were a little label-Gestapo back then."

"Still am," she said proudly.

She smelled it when he opened the door: the scent of linseed oil and old linens. For some reason, it soothed her. He flipped on the lights and she peered around. She hadn't been here since high school, but it still looked the same as it had ten years ago. Warm, comfy, lived in. A worn brown sofa took up the center of the room, and in front of it lay a braided rug that covered natural hardwood floors shot with amber and gold. A hulking wood-burning stove took up half of the back wall.

The cottage was the antithesis of every home she'd ever lived in with her own family, which was half the appeal. Still, she couldn't stop herself from straightening the rug with the toe of her pearly slipper.

"It's not the Ritz, but—"

She waved a hand to stop him. "It's home. I couldn't be happier with the choice."

He looked at her for a long moment and nodded. "I'm glad. I'm going to get some of Cat's clothes for you so you can change. You know where everything is. Make yourself comfy."

"Thanks." She stared after him as he went, vowing to stand up for him the next time Cat bitched about what a pain he was. He'd saved her bacon tonight, allowing her to keep at least a shred of dignity by getting her out of there before she resorted to plate flinging and spittle-filled rants. Part of her wished Cat were there, but in a way, Galen was the perfect person for the job. She didn't want to talk about her feelings or share her gruesome revenge plots. Not yet. Right now it hurt to breathe and she needed to just...be.

She crossed the living room and puttered around the perimeter, reminiscing over the pictures that riddled the walls. Although most were of the Thomas children, she was in quite a few herself. Her gaze fell on one in particular that had her sucking in a sharp breath. Three little girls: one brunette, one blonde, and one with hair that was too orange to be called red mugged for the camera. Cat had her nose pulled up like a pig while she and Becca made fish faces around her, crossing their eyes for good measure.

Damn it, Becs.

She waited for the fury to come, but that emotion seemed to be reserved for Marty. When she thought of Becca, all that came was bone-deep sadness. Twenty years of friendship—no, *sisterhood*—gone in a flash. Over a man who turned out to be less than a man. Over Marty.

"I was thinking they'd be a little musty because she hasn't been up this season yet."

Lacey swiped the tears away and pasted a smile on her face before turning to face Galen. Saved by the bell again, right before she was about to dissolve into a puddle of sad.

"But she kept them in the cedar chest, so they're not bad at all." He crossed the room, holding up a pair of yoga pants and a hoodie. "These okay?"

She took them with a grateful smile. "Perfect. I'll be back in a second."

It wasn't a second, but it was close. When she got into the bathroom and looked at herself in the mirror, wedding updo and makeup still half in effect, far less modestly dressed than she'd realized, she wanted to hide there forever. How mortifying. Always gorgeous Galen had seen her at her worst today, both literally and figuratively. And the slip that hadn't seemed all that revealing when she'd been alone in her bedroom that morning now looked obscene. Thank God The Admiral hadn't seen her get onto Galen's bike like this.

Her thoughts spiraled and suddenly, in spite of her embarrassment over Galen having seen her half naked, she couldn't wait to get back into the living room. The thought of being alone right now made her whole body tense. She tore off the slip and stockings and stuffed them into the trash can before tugging on Cat's laze-around-the-house clothes. After scrubbing her face clean, she yanked the pins from her hair and combed it with her fingers.

By the time she got back to Galen, he'd taken off his jacket and started the stove. He looked up from his perch on a stool by the island in the kitchen. "You hungry? I can make some soup or something."

"Not really."

"Are you just planning to stay one night or did you want me to go to the store and get some groceries to last you a few days?"

"I—" She frowned. In her efforts to not think about her now demolished future, she'd been focused on putting one foot in front of the other. For the first time in her well-ordered life, she had no idea what her plans were. "If I need anything, I'll walk down to the general store tomorrow." He stood, and her stomach pitched. "W-where are you going?"

"Home. You don't need me here watching you cry or whatever it is you planned on spending the night doing."

His smooth baritone took on an edge of nervousness that almost made her feel sorry for him. Almost. But the thought of him leaving her by herself squashed it dead, and she prepared to beg if need be.

"I don't want to cry. I don't want to think. Tomorrow, when it's a little less fresh, I'll do my thinking and crying until I decide how to pick up the pieces. But for right now, what I'd like to do is get piss drunk and forget for a few hours." She took a deep breath and wrung her hands together. "And I'd rather not do it alone."

He hesitated for a long second, but when he nodded and faced her, his dark gaze was warm. "Getting drunk and embracing denial?" His lips quirked into a half grin. "Well then, I'm your man."

• • •

Twenty minutes later they faced off across the coffee table, Lacey on the floor close to the wood-burning stove with her feet curled under her bottom, and Galen on the couch. A bottle of Jack Daniel's sat between them, surrounded by eight shot glasses, some full and some half full.

"Are you sure about this? I've only ever played with beer. Maybe we should use the champagne instead?" Lacey asked, turning a dubious eye to the shooters.

"Are you chickening out?" he asked, making sure his tone was chock full of scorn. He chuckled when her expression clearly indicated she was thinking about it. "Champagne seems a little highbrow for this game. Plus, between the two of us, it ain't gonna get the job done. I can offer you some cooking sherry. It's from last spring, but I'm sure it's fine. Probably."

She wrinkled her nose. "That's okay, I'll pass. We'll stick with the Jack."

He held his fist out for a bump, and she obliged him with a roll of her eyes. Perfect. So long as he was annoying her, she wouldn't cry. It had been more than a decade since he'd hit someone outside the ring, but for some reason, he didn't think he could take even one more tear coming from those haunted eyes without driving back to the reception hall and popping Marty Clemson right in the chops.

Repeatedly.

"So what are the rules of this game?" he asked.

Lacey had taken her hair down from the fussy wedding 'do, and gold curls tumbled over her shoulders, making her wan skin look even more so by contrast. It was priority number one to put some color in those cheeks.

"The game is called I Never. The boys used to beg us to play back in college so they could try and take advantage of us later."

He held up a hand as if to warn her to stay on her side of the table. "I'm flattered. Really. But I'm going to need some time to think it over." That got a chuckle from her, which sent a bolt of satisfaction coursing through him.

"I'll try to control myself. So here's how it works. I'm going to say something that I've never done. If you've never done it, either, it's your turn. If you *have* done it, you drink one of the small shots. If you want to plead the fifth and not answer, you have to drink one of the full shots. Get it?"

"Sounds pretty simple. I'll start," he said.

"Wait, why you?"

"My house, my liquor."

She curled her lip and shook her head. "Geez, what happened to ladies first?"

"I save that mentality for the bedroom. Outside the bedroom, it's an even playing field, so man up."

Her cheeks went pink at that and the fist gripping his gut eased a little. She didn't realize it yet, but she would get through this fine and come out the other side better for it. He'd always felt like her relationship with Marty had been based more on her feelings of friendship and a responsibility toward her parents than anything else. Not exactly the recipe for a knock-your-socks-off love affair. He hadn't been lying when he'd told her this was the best thing that could've happened to her. Clemson wasn't even close to man enough for Lacey. Maybe once she was ready to talk about it, he would lecture her on finding a man who could take care of her right.

Not that it was any of his business.

She cleared her throat and finally responded to his teasing. "The bedroom, very funny."

What was funny was that she'd honed in on that particular phrase. He couldn't stop himself from pushing a little further. "Oh, I'm dead serious, squirt. Just ask around."

Her gaze traveled to his mouth, and her throat worked as she swallowed. Before he could think on that development too hard, she picked up a handful of the cashews they'd commandeered from the kitchen cabinet and lobbed one at him. "Stop trying to embarrass me."

He caught the nut and popped it into his mouth. "Sorry, but you're such an easy mark. Okay, so me first. Let's see. Here's one. I've never…been skydiving before."

Pursing her lips, she thought about that for a second. "I have. On my twenty-first birthday. Craziest thing I've ever done."

He knew that, which was the reason he'd chosen it. If she was determined to get drunk, they might as well get started. He tipped his chin toward the table. "Drink up."

She selected one of the half-filled glasses and tossed back the contents. Her eyes watered as she chased it with a deep pull from a bottle of water. "My turn," she croaked. "I've never…eaten sushi."

He grinned and shook his head. "Me neither. And why would I? Seems like a slap in the face to those poor cavemen who worked long and hard to create fire. Guess that means no drink for me. My turn again. I've never..." He racked his brain for something else he knew about her that might be a little wild. "I've never...gone skinny-dipping."

She sent him a dirty look and picked up another shot. "You are so full of it. In fact, a bunch of us went together in this very lake!"

"True. I'll drink, too, then. I was getting thirsty." He drank his down in one swallow while Lacey stared at hers like it was a cup full of poison. "Well?"

"It's worse because now I know what it's going to taste like," she admitted. She glared at it for a second then straightened her shoulders. "Here's mud in your eye." She managed to get it down easier than the first and grinned triumphantly as she slammed the glass back on the table. "My turn. I've never cheated on a test."

He waited to see if she picked up a drink and rolled his eyes when she didn't. "Of course you haven't." He took a shot and she laughed. He liked the sound of it, so from that point on, he made sure to ham it up.

"I've never...seen a rated X movie," he said, picking up another whiskey.

She shrugged. "Nope."

He shook his head incredulously. "That's sad." He drank.

"I've never had a threesome," she said, raising a challenging brow.

He pretended to mull that one over for a second then grabbed a glass before pausing. "Do I have to do one for each incident or...?"

She gaped, her mouth wide enough for him to see her tonsils. "More than once? Seriously?"

"I'll take that as a no and do the one shot," he said with a grin. Truth was, although he'd had the opportunity a few times when his career was at its high point, he'd only actually gone through with it once. Not his style. He wanted to focus all his energy on that one person and wring out every drop of pleasure from the lady sharing his bed. It was the one way to be sure she came back for more. He watched Lacey refill the glasses in her ordered, precise way, and wondered if Marty had ever blown her mind.

His tongue was loose from the drinks and curiosity burned a hole in his gut. The words were out before he could stop them. "I've never had multiple orgasms with a man before." He didn't take his eyes off her as she set down the bottle.

For a tense moment, he thought she might opt to drink a full shot to avoid answering either way. He'd clearly set her up, and he wouldn't blame her. Instead, she countered in a voice almost too soft to hear.

"I've never had *one* orgasm with a man before."

Chapter Three

The shot glass fell from his suddenly limp fingers and hit the coffee table with a *clunk*.

Well, damn.

It was his turn to gape now. Forget blowing her mind, Marty hadn't been getting Lacey off at all. His earlier assertion that the man was a spineless prick now seemed like an insult to spineless pricks everywhere. He was worse than that. He was a selfish, pathetic, spineless prick.

"And this is the man you picked to marry?" he demanded before he thought better of it. "Why would you want to subject yourself to a lifetime of bad sex?"

Her cheeks flushed and she looked away, toying with the hood string of her sweatshirt. "It wasn't *bad*. It just wasn't... good. Anyway, it wasn't his fault."

"Bullshit." He was surprised at his own vehemence. His instincts bleated out those warnings again, but the haze of liquor relegated them to background noise.

"The problem wasn't Marty, okay? It was me," she blurted. "I...can't do it. It's complicated."

She looked so utterly miserable that he slapped back

the urge to rant about the fucker. Now wasn't the time. Hell, maybe it would never be time, but suddenly he wanted Lacey to know it wasn't complicated. In fact, he could make it all very, very simple.

Blood pumped south, and his cock swelled as images of Lacey sprawled out beneath him filled his head. He plucked up another glass and drank it down. "That one was just because I'm thirsty," he said, and sat back. "Listen, squirt, with every hour that passes, it's becoming more and more obvious to me that you got lucky today finding out what kind of person he really is. You were together how long?"

She held up three fingers. "Almost two years." She looked at her hand and did a double take before using her other hand to fold down her index finger.

Good. She might be too drunk to count, but at least she wasn't crying. "And he still couldn't make you come? That's a lot of time to figure out what makes you tick."

"That's the problem. Nothing makes me tick. My ticker's broken, I think." She picked up the bottle and swirled it absently, pretending to be enthralled with the liquid inside rather than meeting his gaze.

"That's what guys who don't understand how to handle the delicate gears of a clock will tell you. I'm telling you something different. I may be a lot of things, but I'm no liar."

"It wasn't only him, though. There was a guy in college. That was just as ba—" She set the bottle down and seemed to regroup. "I mean, with him, too, I couldn't…yanno."

She waggled her brows until he nodded his understanding, a smile tugging at his lips.

"We tried, believe me. We flipped through the Kama Sutra and picked out some of the positions, but he had an issue with his electrolytes and kept getting cramps." She was totally straight-faced, as if that were the most logical explanation in the world.

"You don't need to be a human pretzel, Lacey. There are dozens, hell, *hundreds* of ways to come without stretching into strange positions."

Her eyes widened. "Hundreds? Are you sure?" Before he could answer, she shook her head. "That doesn't matter, anyway. Sex isn't that important. At least, not as important as companionship, and respect, and —"

"Bullshit," he said again.

She turned slightly unfocused but indignant eyes on him. "You don't think those things are important?"

"Of course they are. But so is sex. Otherwise why not have everyone be just friends? We can all sit around a campfire and sing 'Kumbaya' together and talk about how much we respect each other."

"Don't make fun of me, Galen. Just because we don't agree doesn't mean you're right."

"We don't agree because you have no clue what you're talking about. It's like trying to talk boxing with a lawyer." He couldn't resist another not-so-subtle jab at Marty. "There's no frame of reference for him to work off of. Same goes here for you."

She opened her mouth to argue, but he cut her off, leaning over the table until his face was only a foot from hers. "If you've never had a man trail his fingertips over every inch of your naked body until he figured out what made you squirm…"

The instant dilation of her pupils gave him pause and left his cock twitching. He pressed on, determined to make his point.

"If you've never had a man lick you from your navel to your knees…"

She flicked her tongue out to moisten her lips.

"If you've never had a man slide deep, in and out, until your head tossed on the pillow and you begged for more…" His voice had gone dark and gravelly, and he swallowed hard. "Then how can you possibly understand the importance of sexuality in a relationship?"

The room that had crackled with warmth and comfort a few minutes before felt hot and tense. The silence was thick, broken only by harsh breathing and the hooting of owls in the distance.

"I don't know," she whispered finally, breaking the all but palpable connection between them. "I just don't know." She knocked back a drink and swiped the back of her hand over her mouth.

He sat back, opting to let her off the hook. It wasn't the time to push her on this—or any other—issue. When she realized that she'd dodged a bullet with Marty, maybe he could convince her that she deserved passion in her life. And damned if he didn't want to give her the first taste.

Not tonight, though. She was still hurting, so he forced himself to steer things back to a safer path. "Your turn," he said with what he hoped was an affable smile.

An hour later, the bottle between them was almost—he squinted and tried to bring it into focus—three-quarters of the way empty. They'd ceased any pretense of keeping up the game and had spent the last thirty minutes talking. Not about Lacey's situation but about everything else. Her job as marketing director for her family's law firm, his last fight, and what he planned to do when his boxing days were behind him. At some point as they talked, she'd made her way onto the couch next to him and had burrowed her bare feet under his thighs.

His cell phone vibrated in his pocket and he pulled it out to peer at the text.

Call me.

"I've got to call Cat. You want to talk?"

She shook her head. "Not right now."

He hit the call button and his sister picked up after one ring. "Hey."

"Where'd you end up taking her?"

"The cottage."

"You drove her all the way to the cottage in her wedding dress?"

He paused, wondering how much he should say, and went for a half truth. "No, she, ah, took that off at the reception hall." The buttons and the ripping and the creamy skin and his subsequent boner? Not relevant. "In fact, it's probably still in the back parking lot."

Cat cracked out a shocked laugh. "Woo-hoo! Good for her. I'm going to have to get her a plaque or something to celebrate her total kick-assery for doing that. Did you guys stop and get her a new phone before you dropped her off? I'm worried about her being alone."

"I'm still with her." Cat was quiet for so long, he wondered if the call had been dropped. "Hello?"

"I'm here."

Her suspicious tone made him feel twitchy, so he hurried to explain. "You said it. She didn't want to be alone, and I didn't feel right leaving her."

"You're being nice, right?"

"Of course," he grumbled. "What am I, a monster?"

"Well, should I come there? After dealing with the guests, all the details, and Lacey's mother, I'm stone cold sober now, so I don't mind driving up."

She definitely sounded sober, but she also sounded exhausted. It couldn't have been an easy night holding down the fort and keeping Lacey's family at bay. From what he knew of her, Rowena Garrity was one tough bitch. "I don't think you need to. We're managing fine, and she'll need you more tomorrow, I'm sure."

"How is she holding up so far?"

He snuck a glance at Lacey. Her head had lolled to the side. Light snores trembled on her lips and he resisted the urge to run his thumb across the plump bottom one. "She's good, considering."

"Does she want to talk to me?"

"She's sleeping right now. I'll have her call you in the morning."

"It's only eight o'clock at night," she protested. "Wait, are you guys drunk?"

"Her, totally. Me…mostly."

She chuckled on the other end of the line. "Good. She's so uptight sometimes, I was afraid she wouldn't let herself have a day to break down a little. I was half thinking she'd be in a hotel somewhere writing apology letters to the wedding guests and re-mapping her future out on a spreadsheet or whatever." She paused. "Listen, I'm sorry I doubted you. I'm sure you're doing a great job, and I feel a lot better knowing she's got someone there looking out for her."

They said their good-byes and he disconnected, setting the phone on the coffee table.

Lacey stirred, opening her eyes. "Cat worried?"

He nodded. "Yeah, but I told her you were handling it like a champ."

She used the arm of the couch to drag herself into a sitting position. "You really think so? Because it sure doesn't feel that way."

Her hair was sticking out in all directions and he reached out to pat it into place. "I do."

When he pulled back, she clutched his hand to her cheek

and murmured, "Thanks again for all of this."

He allowed himself to stroke the soft skin with his finger for a second before pulling away. "No sweat. You ready to get some sleep?"

"Not yet. Please?"

"It's early, so I'm good to stay up for a while if you are."

"What time is it?"

"Not even nine o'clock."

Her eyes clouded with sadness and she shook her head. "Nine o'clock. That's what time the limo was supposed to pick us up."

"What do you mean?"

"Marty and me. We were supposed to leave for our honeymoon late tonight. Hey! There's one for I Never." She bent forward, and this time she didn't even bother with the glass. "I've never been on an amazing vacation to Puerto Rico," she said, and took a shot straight from the bottle, but she didn't stop there, thrusting it in the air for emphasis. "On the beach, with sugar-white sand and aquamarine water. And mojitos with umbrellas in them instead of this crap."

Her tone was incongruously jovial and he knew she'd reached point break. She moved to drink more of "that crap" but he stayed her hand.

"No more. You're going to make yourself sick."

The borderline hysteria faded from her eyes and she let him take the bottle. "I'm already sick," she mumbled, absently mopping up a few spilled drops of whiskey with the sleeve of her shirt.

He set the bottle on the table and gave her arm a tug until she toppled into his chest. "It's going to get better. I promise you," he whispered into her sweet-smelling hair.

"I know it will. But right now, it blows. I've never been on a real trip without my parents. I was so excited. It felt so decadent and fun. I thought…"

"You thought?"

"I thought I could be someone else for a couple of weeks. And maybe Marty could be someone else, too. We could do all the fun, wild things we—well, at least, I—imagined doing. I know that sounds so stupid."

The thought hit him like an oncoming bus, and no matter how hard he tried to squash it, his liquor-soaked brain wouldn't let it go. He pushed her away. "Let's play truth or dare."

"Wait, wha?" Visibly baffled by the abrupt change in subject, she stared at him, a question in her eyes.

"Truth or dare. Let's play," he pressed.

She held up her hands in surrender. "Uh, okay."

"I'll go first. Do you want truth or dare?" He tried not to let the importance of her answer show on his face, but it was all riding on this. If he truly wanted to help her—and God help him, but for some strange reason, he did—he needed to set her free. Over the past few hours, he had realized how much she deserved that, and he wouldn't rest easy until he'd done it. He was going to find a way to show her what she'd missed living under her parents' thumbs. If only she'd let him…

She finally met his gaze after a long pause, fire lighting her eyes, and he knew her answer before she even spoke.

"Dare."

Chapter Four

Sunlight streamed in through the window, like red knives piercing her closed lids. Lacey rolled to her side to escape it, wincing as her knee connected with something harder than itself.

"*Oof.* What the hell?" a low, male voice hissed.

She lurched into a sitting position, regretting it instantly as pain exploded in her temples and the whole room began to spin. Clutching at her aching head, she turned to see Galen stretched out on the bed next to her.

"Sorry," he said through gritted teeth. "It's just, when you gave me that nice little wakeup kick to the Johnson, you grazed my nuts. Makes it hard to be polite."

He sat up, sucking long breaths in through his nose and blowing them out his mouth, moving the sheet in the process. His broad shoulders came into view, and she found herself needing to do the whole breathing thing, too. Man, he was fit. His traps were thick and strong. Hard-looking, like—

Oh my God. I kneed him in the wiener. And oh my frigging God, it was like stone.

The gauzy white curtains across the room fluttered in

the balmy breeze, inviting and coy. So unlike the curtains in the Thomas family cabin. Memories from the previous night battered around in her mind until she settled on the only one that mattered right now.

They'd done it. They'd really done it.

"I dare you to go on your honeymoon without him," Galen had said last night. "I'll even go with you to keep you company. I could use the rest. I just came off a big fight, and my organs haven't settled back into their proper places yet. You'd be doing me a favor."

"You're insane!" Even as tipsy as she'd been, it had taken her almost twenty minutes to talk herself into it. She'd tossed up every roadblock she could think of at first, ticking them off on her fingers as she went, ending with, "The flight's probably sold out by now and you don't have a ticket."

"Well, if Marty doesn't show up, then they'll obviously have an open seat for standbys," he'd said, a challenging gleam in his eye.

They'd gone to her apartment to pick up her bags and then went straight to the airport. By the time their flight was called a couple hours later, though, she'd been as sober as a nun and had almost backed out. Galen must have seen it coming, because he had leaned in close to whisper, "Bock. Bock."

For a long moment, she'd just gaped at him. "Seriously? You're seriously going to make chicken noises at me? What are we, ten?"

He'd just folded his arms over his chest and grinned.

"Last call for all passengers on flight seventeen fifty-six to San Juan, Puerto Rico," the ticket agent had squawked through the loudspeaker.

"What's it going to be, squirt?"

Maybe it had been the *bock*-ing. Maybe it was that stupid

nickname that he wouldn't let die. Or maybe it was that, when she had gone through her alternatives one last time, the thought of staying home and dealing with the aftermath of the wedding just yet was too much to bear. Whatever it was, she'd gotten on that plane.

And now she was on her honeymoon with Galen Thomas.

Panic threw a splash of nausea into the pitching cauldron of noxious brew that was her stomach, and she groaned.

"It's okay. It's going to be fine." His words and the awkward pat on her shoulder barely registered as she rolled off the bed and stood, scrabbling for the headboard when the room tilted.

When she thought she could stand it, she opened her eyes, made her way over to the window, and pushed the curtain aside.

"I can't believe we're here," she whispered. When they'd arrived in the wee hours that morning, it had still been dark, and after having more drinks on the plane to bolster her waning courage, neither of them had been able to muster up the energy to do more than fall into the only made-up bed in the villa. She stared out at paradise for a long moment and then turned to take in the room—the wash of paint the color of ripe peaches and the sparse, cream-colored wicker furniture—as what had started out as a dare suddenly became very real.

Her partner in crime scrubbed a hand over his wickedly handsome face before grinning at her. "Welcome to Puerto Rico."

Terror joined what was left of yesterday's libations and sent her stomach lurching. She booked it to the adjacent bathroom and retched.

Ten endless minutes later, her aching stomach was finally empty and she stood under the warm spray in the shower.

Every time her thoughts veered to the topic of Marty, Becca, or even Galen, her brain started to hurt, so she steadfastly refused to think about anything but the mundane task of lathering, rinsing, and repeating. When she stepped out a short while later, her stomach had settled, and the hot shower had downgraded her headache from ghastly to uncomfortable.

She ran a plush towel over the fogged mirror and groaned at the bloodshot eyes staring back at her. She'd done something crazy last night. Something totally out of character. And here she was, a married woman in Puerto Rico with a man who was more childhood crush than friend. A man who made her feel too much and do crazy, out of character things. So now what?

Now she had to go out and talk to Galen, and explain why they had to leave. Or, why *she* did, at least. He could stay if he wanted. He had bought his own ticket, and since the villa was already paid for, someone might as well enjoy it. Maybe he'd meet a sexy *señorita*—

Her newly settled tummy pitched at the thought. What the heck was the matter with her? From the second she'd laid eyes on him twenty years ago, she'd known one thing. He would never see her as more than his sister's irritating friend. He was...everything. Gorgeous and funny and smart and strong. And she was still just the other slice of white bread. A flavorless afterthought. A foil for the deliciousness inside. Not remarkable enough for a boy who crackled with life like Galen Thomas.

She'd accepted that as fact early on and had relegated her feelings to the deepest corner of her heart, never sharing them. Not even with Cat or Becca. Eventually, she'd learned to live with the sting of standing by while he paraded around the latest cheerleader in his life, clueless to her pain. And eventually, she'd moved on and lived her own life, engaging in a few awkward relationships with guys more her speed, despite the floopy feeling she still got in her gut whenever he was around. And then she ended up with Marty. Surely, after all this time, her heart should have gotten the memo? It was ridiculous, given the total lack of encouragement on his end. In fact, he'd gone out of his way to discourage her attention at every turn, teasing her mercilessly, debating with her over anything and everything, baiting her into petty arguments.

Until yesterday.

Yesterday, he'd been sweet, and thoughtful, and plain perfect. He'd come to her rescue like…like a knight on shining Harley. She snort-laughed at the ludicrous thought and picked up her comb. Leave it to her to romanticize a nice gesture. He'd done nothing more than help out his sister's friend. No need to read into it more deeply than that. He was probably out there right now, mired in regret, and ready to gnaw off his own limb to escape the bear trap he'd found himself in. He'd be ecstatic when she let him off the hook.

After a few swipes with the comb, she tugged her hair into a loose knot and clipped it, then slicked on some lip gloss. She pulled on the tank top and boxers she'd slept in and turned toward the door. Time to convince him she was okay, and his duty was done. Pasting on a smile, she stepped into the bedroom, but he was nowhere to be found. Music drifted from the living room, and she followed the strains of the salsa into the suite's main room.

"Hey there. Feel better?"

The speech she'd planned died on her lips, unspoken as she took in the scene before her. Galen sat in a lounge chair out on the terrace in board shorts and nothing else. His swarthy skin gleamed in the sunlight, the dips and valleys of his muscles so cut and defined that they could've been drawn on with a Sharpie.

"Lacey?"

She cleared her throat, dragging her gaze upward to meet his. "Y-yeah?"

"You okay?"

"Yep. You're hot." Her cheeks burned. "I mean…it's hot. Out here. So that's why I'm, yanno…hot." She fanned her cheeks for good measure. *Brilliant.*

His dark eyes danced with mirth. "So, now that we've established that Puerto Rico is warm, how are you feeling?"

She looked away. "I'm better, thanks."

"I ordered some breakfast. Just fruit, yogurt, and some toast. I didn't think your stomach could handle much else." He gestured to the spread in front of him. "Sit and eat, and then we can talk. You want coffee?"

She stepped through the French doors and onto the white tiled floor. The warm breeze flirted with the wisps of hair around her face, and she sighed.

"It's so beautiful here."

In spite of the music playing in the background, she could hear the ocean lapping at the shore only a hundred yards away. She walked the length of the patio, around a small swimming pool, until she could see it. Gorgeous. Caribbean blue, so pure it didn't seem real. Her throat went tight with regret.

"I can't stay, though," she whispered, then faced Galen. "I can't stay," she repeated, louder this time for his benefit.

His face gave away nothing, but he stood and pulled out a chair for her. "Come here."

She doubted she could eat, but she sat anyway. He flipped over her mug and poured her some coffee.

"They didn't give us cream. I think we have to order American coffee if we want it next time."

Next time.

"That's okay, I like it like this. But I was serious, Galen.

There won't be a next time. I need to borrow your phone and make arrangements to go home. My parents are probably a wreck. This was totally irresponsible of me, and I have to make it right."

He set his cup down and met her gaze. "Why?"

"What do you mean, why?"

"I mean, you didn't fuck everything up. Marty did. So why do you have to make it right? You didn't do anything wrong."

Easy for him to say. In spite of her mother's feelings on the subject, once her dad got wind of what had happened, there was no way he would allow the merger to go forward until she talked to him. He might have been something of an absentee father, but he wouldn't take kindly to someone mistreating his little girl this way. And there was still The Admiral to deal with.

She sighed. "There are people to call and apologies to be made. I can't hide in a bubble while everything goes to pot around me. This isn't two people deciding to call it quits. We have a merger in the works here, too. My father will pull the plug on the whole thing in a misguided effort to protect me. The merger is a good thing for both firms, and I don't want it on my conscience that it didn't pan out. Everyone shouldn't be punished because Marty couldn't keep it in his pants. I've got to go and talk to my dad and the board and work this through."

His eyes widened incredulously. "Are you kidding me? Your husband banged your bridesmaid on your wedding day, and you think you should be expected to deal with PR issues and play Miss Manners right this second? Come on, Lacey, even your mother couldn't expect that."

The barb about her mother stung, but he had reasons for his animosity. Growing up, The Admiral had never gotten used to her friendship with the less affluent, wild "Thomas girl." The Thomases had inherited the cheapest house in their pricey neighborhood from a distant aunt, and Lacey's mother had never let anyone forget it. Kitty and Bill didn't give a rat's ass, though, God love them, and they never put a dime into improving it. Instead, they scrimped and saved to afford their cottage on the lake.

In spite of her mother's desperate attempts to keep the girls apart, Lacey's friendship with Cat was the one thing Lacey wouldn't budge on. Her mother could pick out her clothes, make her change schools, and could even try to pick her boyfriends. But Cat was too precious to lose. She was a beam of light in the perpetual smog of Lacey's dreary days. The person who taught her how to kiss by demonstrating on a pillow, and got her to sing into a brush in front of the mirror. If not for her, sometimes Lacey thought she would've withered up and died.

And she certainly had no delusions about her mother. "You'd be surprised what my mother expects."

"I guess I misspoke. What I meant was, it's not reasonable to ask that of you." He reached out and covered her hand with his own. "Stay."

His fingers were warm on her wrist. She swallowed hard as electricity pulsed between them. "I don't get it. W-why is it so important?"

"Because I want you to."

"You don't even like me."

He shoved himself back from the table and stood. "That's the last time I want to hear that," he said, a warning in his tone. Two steps brought him to her side, towering over her. He pulled her to her feet and she wound up nose to flat male nipple.

She moistened her suddenly dry lips. "Well, we haven't exactly been great friends all these years."

"We're friends now, okay? I wouldn't be here if we weren't. Besides, what guy hangs out with his little sister's bestie? You guys were three years behind me. That would've been creepy. But we're adults now. And hey?" Mercifully, he nudged her chin up so her gaze was no longer locked on that tempting chest of his. "I'm sorry it took me so long to recognize that. When I moved out to the city to train, I thought when I got back everything would still be the same. I guess I fell back into the old routine of yanking your chain without really taking into account that you'd grown up. In my defense, once you started dating Marty, it was easy, what with all the ammunition."

His pearly teeth flashed in a wolfish grin that she found herself returning. "I'm starting to wonder if maybe I was drugged or something. He is sort of a weird choice," she admitted ruefully. In fact, as she thought of him now, even the anger had started to fade.

Galen nodded. "See what I mean? After a couple weeks here, you're going to go home as convinced as I am that this was all for the best."

"Maybe it's more than that, though." She paused, her throat aching. "I never in a million years thought Becca would do this to me." Her voice cracked on the end, and she cursed herself for being such a wimp. But damn, it hurt. "Was it my fault, Galen? Did I do something to make this happen?"

"No. Not even a little bit. Hell, even if you were a nightmare of a friend and a terrible fiancée, it wouldn't be your fault. He should've broken up with you if he didn't want you."

She laughed bitterly. "Thanks loads."

"You didn't let me finish." He brushed away the tears on her cheeks with his thumb. "Thing is? I've known you a long time, and I know for a fact you were neither of those things.

You were a great friend to Becca and a better woman than a guy like Marty could ever hope for. They don't deserve you. Not him, and not her."

She sniffled and swiped a hand over her eyes. "You say that, but you don't even li—"

"Stop that. I like you fine. Hell, more than fine." He tucked a stray strand of hair behind her ear, but he hesitated for a beat too long, tracing the shell with his forefinger. Just that simple touch sent a shiver through her, and she pulled back.

"Lacey, I—"

The theme song from *Rocky* blared from the pocket of his shorts. He lowered his hand and stepped back. "That's Cat." He rolled his eyes. "And so you know, I didn't program that song in—she did."

Lacey nodded dumbly and stepped back, grateful for the reprieve. She didn't know what kind of strange voodoo was going on with Galen, but this seemingly newfound awareness on his part was driving her nutty. How she felt about him had always been one-sided. Now the chemistry was crackling from all angles, and it scared the crap out of her.

Not that it mattered. Sure, it had hurt that Marty cheated. And sure, she was embarrassed and angry that someone she cared about had broken her trust. But even though she'd come to the not-so-stunning realization that she hadn't been in love with him—and hadn't been able to admit to herself until, underneath all the anger, she'd felt a nugget of relief yesterday in the linen closet—she was still a married woman. At least for as long as it took to get the annulment papers worked out. Just because he was a cheater didn't mean she had to join him in the gutter. Dimly, she heard Galen saying his good-byes to his sister.

"How is everything going?" she asked as he disconnected. "Didn't she want to talk to me?"

"Nope. She said to call her later. She contacted your mom and dad to let them know you came to Puerto Rico, so that's taken care of."

Lacey had forgotten that they'd called Cat last night to tell her their plan. Her friend had been all for it. Her only gripe was that she couldn't join them because of the spring collection she had to finish putting together at work.

As Lacey contemplated what the call between Cat and her mother must have been like, she found herself grateful that she'd smashed her own phone to smithereens at the reception hall. She couldn't imagine having that conversation right now.

"She also said that Marty's been looking for you. She didn't tell him where you were, but he wants you to call him."

She snorted, and he shrugged.

"I'm only the messenger. For what it's worth, Cat agrees with me one hundred percent. We both think you should stay."

Nerves sent her heart pounding as she finally allowed herself to seriously consider that option. Could she do it? Throw caution to the wind and leave the mess of her ill-fated marriage to molder while she dove headlong into Puerto Rico? "I have to call my lawyer," she hedged. "See about getting an annulment in the works." It was a feeble argument. It would take one phone call to get the ball rolling and months to get through the red tape. She didn't really need to go home for that. "And my dad. I wouldn't put it past him to do something rash come Monday morning, and I can't allow that."

"Don't think about me, or Cat, or Marty. Don't think about your parents or what their snobby country club friends will say or what the board wants. What do *you* want to do, Lacey?" His eyes delved deep, searching for something she couldn't name. She felt like she was standing on a precipice, and no matter which way she turned, she was going down hard. Changes were brewing, and it was up to her to navigate her own ship for once.

The question hung between them like prickly vines, and in the center, the answer dangled before her like a fat, ripe berry ready to drop. She wanted to stay. But if she did—and with Galen, no less—would she ever be able to fit back into the square-shaped hole she'd left behind?

And more importantly, did she even want to?

• • •

Galen could almost hear the slap of skin on skin as she wrestled with herself. He'd done his part and had made a vow to himself that he wouldn't say another word. She needed to step up to the ropes here and decide—in or out. He wasn't going to be another in the long line of puppeteers yanking her strings.

Just when he thought she was going to bail for the second time in twenty-four hours, she shocked him. Steeling her shoulders, she tipped her chin to meet his gaze. "Okay. I'll stay. *If* I can talk my dad down some."

It was what he wanted, so the fear nipping at the heels of his euphoria was a little confusing. He didn't let on, though. She was one flimsy excuse from changing her mind, and he wasn't about to give it to her. Why should being in close quarters with her scare him, anyway? He was a big boy, and he could handle it, even if he had to spend the next two weeks taking cold showers in order to do it.

He filed that problem under "shit to deal with later" and gave her a thumbs-up. "Excellent. Let's eat, then you can call your lawyer and your father while I pack a bag. We're going to the beach."

She popped off a snotty salute. "Yes sir."

They made short work of their light meal, and he handed his phone over so she could make her calls. He packed quickly and had just zipped the beach bag closed when she came into the bedroom a short while later, the crease in her brow less pronounced. That was a good sign.

"How did it go?"

"With my lawyer? Fine. He's making some calls and getting things rolling. With my father?" She shrugged, handing his phone to him. "Better than I expected, actually. He's furious with Marty, but he agreed to wait until I got back to make any decisions about the merger. Then he told me I'd better call my mother, because she's flipping out. I made him promise not to give her this number and asked him to try to calm her down. He's going to do his best."

"Great. You look less stressed already."

"I feel a little better. Like I can unplug for a while and maybe everything won't fall apart around me worse than it already has."

Now that he'd taken responsibility for her, he was determined to buttress the walls around her and even more determined to follow through and help her figure out who she was and what she wanted to do next with her life. It was a dangerous line to walk because, over the course of one day, he was already scarily attracted to her. As they spent more time together, he had the sneaking suspicion he was only going to want her more.

"Let's hit the beach," he said.

She nodded, but held out her hand for the bag. "Did you pack towels?"

"Of course."

"Sunblock?"

"Yep." He crossed his arms over his chest as she spent the next ten minutes pawing through the bag and reorganizing everything he'd packed. "You might be surprised to know that I'm a grown man who *has* packed a bag a time or two in his day."

"I know that, but it's better to spend a few minutes double-checking than getting down to the beach and realizing we forgot something."

She must have heard the prissy tone in her voice because her cheeks turned pink and she zipped the bag closed. "Let's just go."

He chuckled and they stepped out the front door, locking it behind them. Lacey was double-checking the lock when a heavily accented voice called from down the pathway.

"Mr. and Mrs. Clemson?" A round young man dressed in a porter's uniform huffed his way up the incline from the sprawling white building that acted as a reception and dining area for the all-villa resort.

Lacey stiffened, but Galen took her arm. "That's us." No point in making her explain the confusing *Jerry Springer*-esque situation to a stranger.

"I have some messages for you that were left with the front desk. Your mother would like you to call her as soon as possible. They started coming in early this morning, but we try not to bother guests until at least ten a.m. unless it's a family emergency."

He wouldn't meet her gaze as he handed over a pile of creamy white paper, and Lacey took it with a frown. "Thank you."

The porter swiped an arm over his sweaty brow and smiled. "No problem."

Given his size and the redness of his face, it had clearly been a problem. Galen pulled a ten out of his pocket. "Thanks"—he glanced at the name tag—"Jesus. The missus and I appreciate it."

Jesus smiled his thanks, pocketed the cash, and turned to start his slow descent back down the hill. Galen turned to Lacey, whose frown was deepening as she read.

"What is it?"

"From my mother." She handed him the pile and pressed two fingers to her temple to rub.

He hadn't read a word of it, and he was already annoyed. In a matter of one minute, Rowena had ratcheted up Lacey's anxiety tenfold and it had him half wishing a house would fall on her. When he started reading, the half wish ramped up to burning desire.

Lacey—
Call me IMMEDIATELY. Do not make another move until you contact me.
—Mother.

He flipped to the next one.

Lacey—
Call me this instant. You're behaving like a child.
—Mother

The next:

Take a day to sulk, pick yourself up by your bootstraps, and plan to return home tomorrow. There are multiple important matters that need your attention.
I will expect a call tomorrow with your flight number so I can send a driver to collect you at the airport.

Apparently, the salutations were no longer needed.

He fanned out the stack, and she shook her head. There were three more and, if the pattern held, they would only be increasingly hostile.

"Listen, I don't think you should—"

She held up a hand. "Say no more. I agree. I'm done with her for the time being." She took a deep breath and crumpled them into a ball. "Lead me to that beach, sir. I need some cooling off."

She looked so strong in that moment, he wanted to pump his fist or give her a high five, but he held back. When he was preparing for a big fight, his trainer would take him mountain climbing to build up his hand strength and endurance. Max's favorite piece of advice? Don't look down until you reach the summit. Galen had asked why, thinking Max would give him some inspirational shit about the satisfaction of seeing how far he'd come at the end or something. Instead, Max had snorted, "Because it's fucking scary."

This was another small step toward independence for Lacey, and he wasn't about to call too much attention to it, because it was definitely scary for her.

But inside? Inside he was beaming with pride.

• • •

An hour later, Galen found himself sitting under an umbrella on a lounge chair, seriously questioning his sanity. What the hell had he been thinking taking her to the beach? It had been bad enough with her prancing around in boxer shorts and a tank top, but this was ridiculous. She'd started off in some sort of muumuu-type cover-up, but after twenty minutes in the sultry heat, she'd seemed to gather her courage and had shucked it off. He, along with every other guy on that spit of beach, had nearly swallowed his tongue.

She stood before him now against the backdrop of crystal blue water in a nefarious white string bikini. Four triangles of cloth clung to her with no more aid than a slender chain on each curve of hip and one looped around her neck. It was enough to rock his socks off.

"Does it look stupid?" She wrapped her arms around her waist, which only succeeded in pressing her breasts together, plumping them against the edge of her suit, which, in turn, sent something plumping against his. "It looks stupid. I'm going to go to the gift shop and get a tank suit. I don't know what I was thinking."

She retrieved her cover-up and was in the process of tugging it back on by the time he finally trusted himself to speak. "Don't."

She paused and met his gaze. "I look silly. This isn't me. I'm not ballsy enough to pull this off." She bit her lip and turned away. "I just wanted..."

"I know what you wanted." He would've stood, but his physiological response to her state of undress made that impossible unless he wanted to get himself arrested for indecent exposure. "You wanted to let go, have some fun, do something different and exciting." The genuine sadness in her eyes kept him from adding, *And for the record, I'm different and exciting.*

She clutched the brightly patterned cloth more tightly in her hands. "Yeah."

"So I don't know why you're trying to talk yourself out of it now. The hard stuff is over. You dumped the groom, ran out on your wedding reception, and jumped on the back of a Harley in your slip. Then you got drunk and flew to Puerto Rico with your best friend's older brother, who, incidentally, thinks you look smoking hot. Who's got more balls than you?" he asked, allowing some annoyance to trickle into his tone. His baiting her was terra firma for them both. Hopefully the familiarity of it would remind her that he was, and always had been, a straight shooter. He wasn't blowing smoke up her ass here. A lot of people in her shoes would've crumbled after yesterday, but she'd handled that lights-out blow to the chin better than most of the heavyweights he'd fought.

Her eyes went so wide, she could've been a cartoon. "Y-You think I look hot?" Her wringing hands went limp and her cover-up fell to the sand.

He considered backpedaling rather than revealing exactly how much she affected him, but one look at the hope on her face killed that notion. Instead, he played it matter-of-fact. "I don't think it, squirt. I know it. It's like water's wet, the sky is blue, Lacey looks fine as hell in her bikini." He shrugged. "Facts are facts. You've gotta get some confidence working because I think your view of yourself is skewed. Fake it until you make it."

She lifted her hands to cross them over her midsection again, but then froze, letting them drop to her sides. Sucking in a deep breath, she nodded, then snagged the cover-up. "I'll try," she said, and folded it into a neat little square before setting it on her chair.

His little head thanked him for the return of the visual smorgasbord while his big head cursed him for not minding his own damned business. He'd put himself in a terrible spot here. Sure, he wanted to make her feel better, but at this rate, he was going to have a *Guinness Book*–worthy case of blue balls.

"Want to go for a swim?" he asked, more out of self-preservation than anything. Cold water would be a godsend right now.

"I do, but most of my skin hasn't seen the sun since summer, and some of these parts have *never* seen it." She gestured to the smooth expanse of flat stomach. "I've got to slather on SPF five thousand until I get a base tan."

He jammed a hand into the duffel bag he'd packed and pulled out the bottle of sunscreen.

"Smart thinking." Only now he had to watch her apply it. He tossed it to her, and then settled back against the chair as if he were going to relax a while. As she uncapped the bottle and poured some lotion into her palm, he pinched his eyes closed. He would *not* think about her working that lotion over his cock until he came. He would *not* imagine bending her over and massaging it into her ass cheeks, his fingers trailing closer and closer to the heat between her thighs until she begged for more. He would not look, because that would only make it w—

His lids lifted of their own accord, and he heard himself ask, "Do you need help with your back?"

"Nope, I already got it. I do yoga so I'm super flexible."

He bit back a groan. He definitely could've done without that little nugget of information. Now not only could he visualize them having wild monkey sex, he could also imagine doing it in some very creative positions.

She turned and jogged toward the ocean. He found himself mesmerized by the swing of her hips. "You coming?" she called over her shoulder.

Not yet, but that could be arranged in short order.

Damn, he was a perv. He really needed to do something about that. "Right behind you."

She stopped at the edge of the water and dipped a careful toe in. Then she ran straight into the spray with reckless abandon, her delighted laughter spurring him to his feet. He covertly adjusted his man-junk as best he could and stood. There were at least a dozen other women reclined on colorful beach towels, similarly clothed, but he couldn't tear his eyes away from Lacey.

By the time he reached the water, she was submerged up

to her neck. He thanked God for small favors. The cool ocean lapped at his ankles as he watched her swim. Behind her, a monster wave was swelling. He cupped his hands around his mouth and shouted, "Incoming!"

She turned her head and squealed, paddling toward him. At first he thought she was afraid and started toward her, but then he realized she was laughing. Right as the wave crested, she stretched her arms straight in front of her and came blasting his way, skimming across the top of the water like she was resting on a surfboard. The immense power of the ocean and the exhilaration on her face sent his heart pounding. The wave finally deposited her in a heap at his feet. The back of her white bikini bottoms was covered in mud and her top was...

Gone.

"That was so much fun. Come do one with me!" She was lying in the shallow water on her stomach and rose to a kneel before he could stop her. Her full breasts were streaked with wet sand, but it didn't hide the twin hard peaks beckoning him. The blood drained from his brain, all headed south, and words wouldn't come. He did manage to step closer, blocking her from the sun worshippers on the shore behind him.

Her smile dimmed. "What's the matter? You don't like salt water?"

"I like it fine." His voice was gritty and he cleared his throat. "But you need to get back all the way in and lie on your stomach."

She shot him a puzzled glance and then followed his gaze downward. Letting out a strangled "*Gack!*" she didn't so much lay back down as she did pitch forward into the shallow water, flat on her face. She came up sputtering and spat out a mouthful of sand before slapping her hands over her breasts. Frantically, she squirmed toward deeper water, but down two working appendages and fighting the incoming waves, she wasn't getting anywhere.

A child's giggles broke the spell Lacey's naked breasts had weaved over him, and he realized a family was entering the water right next to them. Dropping to his knees in front of her, he tugged her up into an embrace, pressing her chest to his. "Wrap your arms around me," he said against her ear. "I'm going to stand and carry you out farther so no one can see you. Then, I'm going to go back to shore and get your cover-up, all right?"

She burrowed her head into the crook of his neck and nodded. There was a long pause and then she released her breasts to snake her arms around his neck. He sucked in a breath as her softness smashed against his hardness. The cool slide of her skin against his sent a sizzle of lust through him, so strong he nearly toppled over.

"This is so mortifying. This is why I don't do anything wild or crazy. I suck at it. One bikini in my whole life and look what happens. Even when we were young, your sister used to say I was the kiss of death because whenever she convinced me to do something fun, I always ended up getting us caught or screwing it up somehow."

He focused on her panicked babbling and held onto her thighs to stabilize her.

"You okay? Am I too heavy?"

"Nope, I needed to adjust my grip, is all." He stood, lifting her with him, and she wrapped her legs around his waist. He hadn't thought that far ahead and groaned as she straddled him, lining her pubic bone directly against the throbbing heat of his dick. She stiffened in his arms and gasped, the babbling coming to a screeching halt. His starving brain cast around fruitlessly for another way to carry her, but this was the only way to preserve her modesty, which in turn obliterated his.

When the water was deep enough to swim in, the strength of the waves began to rock her body against his in a torturous rhythm. The need to rock back, grinding into her softness, was so strong he had to stop for a second and get a grip. That's when he felt it. The subtle shift of her hips as her body pressed closer, pulsing against his, as if driven by instinct. She clutched at his shoulders, burrowing closer, her nipples pebbling against his chest. The blast of want hit him so hard, he had to grit his teeth to keep from groaning.

Clutching at her thighs, he anchored her still. "Stop wriggling," he said. His voice was low, gruff, and strained.

She froze. "S-sorry."

The warm puff of air against his ear and the break in her voice almost threw him right over the edge. What would Little Lacey Garrity do if he stripped aside those tiny bikini bottoms and buried himself in her again and again until she screamed?

Not the plan, asshole.

He took a steadying breath and strode purposefully into the surf, reciting his times tables as he went. He wouldn't think about how soft her breasts were, pillowed against him. Or how her tight little nipples were branding his chest. Or how they'd looked in the morning sunshine, pouty, glistening with ocean water, begging for his tongue.

"Okay, good enough," he announced abruptly, and released her, stepping back like she was on fire.

She covered her breasts again, dipping low until she was immersed in the blue water.

He averted his gaze and cleared his throat. "We're the only ones out this far, so if you turn to face the open ocean, no one will see," he said, his voice almost guttural now. Too bad. He didn't want to shock her, but he was only flesh and blood, and there was nothing he could do about it.

She didn't respond to his suggestion and wouldn't look

at him.

"Lacey?" Still nothing. Shit. She was upset. He struggled to find words over the cacophony of his roaring libido. "It's no big deal. Don't let this derail you. You came here to let loose, to get away from the drama at home. Now you have a funny story to tell." He tipped her chin so she had no choice but to look at him. "Talk to me, squirt."

When she finally met his gaze, he wished she hadn't. Her pupils were dilated, her nostrils flaring lightly as she struggled for air. The pulse in her neck fluttered, and he stared at it, overcome with the desire to close his teeth over the delicate skin there. The adrenaline rush of the situation may have intensified her feelings, but one thing was clear that hadn't been the night before. Her body's reaction to him wasn't a fluke. She was as hot for him as he was for her.

Bad news for Lacey because, up until that moment, he'd relegated himself to the role of unofficial guardian. But now that he knew the vibe he'd felt from her last night was more than just the alcohol and stress of the situation—now that he knew she wanted him for real?

It was on.

Chapter Five

"You're a married woman," she told herself. "At least until the annulment." Lacey watched her reflection, waiting for it to roll its eyes at her stern reminder.

She muffled a groan. Crap. She was in big trouble. No. Huge, ginormous, major trouble, because she was madly in lust with her best friend's brother and it was so not okay. She bent at the waist and rubbed the towel vigorously over her hair. Just the feel of Galen's hard body against hers had her senses rioting in a way that even the whole tamale with Marty hadn't. If she wasn't sure she'd made a mistake in her choice of husbands before, she was sure of it now.

Was that what it was supposed to feel like? Wild and crazy and like you would do anything...anything at all for another taste? Or was it the sand and sun coupled with her first taste of real freedom? She'd had some during college, but since her parents had insisted she go to a posh school only forty minutes from home, even that had been tempered by their influence. Now she was free to do whatever she wanted, whenever she wanted, and there was no one to judge her for it.

Except Galen.

She straightened and hung the towel on the hook behind her. Somehow, despite the jabs they'd exchanged over the years, she got the distinct feeling they were in a judgment-free zone. She could act a fool, and he would stand back, watch, and smile. She could drink and dance and act crazy, and he'd be fine with that. Was his only motive to try and help her through this transition, encouraging her to let go a little and enjoy this trip? Or was there more to it? If the hot ridge in his bathing suit had been any indication, she would have to guess the latter.

She suppressed a shiver and tugged her dress over her head. Why now? Why after all these years had he finally decided to notice her?

"Save me some hot water," he called through the door.

If she'd had the balls he gave her credit for, she would've suggested he join her next time. But she didn't, and she wouldn't. Instead she smoothed the skirt of her cotton sundress and opened the door. "I've been out for ten minutes now. I was getting changed." She stepped into the bedroom and gestured to the bathroom door. "It's all yours. Make sure you wipe out the drain when you're done. And hang up your towel."

He smirked and flicked a lighting-fast hand out, snapping said towel at her bare toes.

"Hey!" she squealed and jumped back.

"Don't take that bossy tone with me. I'm telling you right now, I'm going to leave stuff everywhere. Toilet seat up, towels on the floor, cap off the milk." He tugged his T-shirt over his head and dropped in on the floor. "We need to break you of this control freakiness, and this is the perfect time to learn how to go with the flow and just let things happen."

Inexplicably, his harmless words felt as weighty as the pressure in her belly. She tried not to stare at him but failed miserably. His board shorts hung low, clinging to his lean hips. She helplessly followed the trail of hair leading from his navel downward…

"If I didn't know better, I'd think you never saw a half-naked man before, squirt." His voice had dropped to almost a whisper, and even the childish nickname felt like a caress.

"I have," she protested and took another step back. "Plenty of times." Okay, she might have exaggerated a bit, but he didn't need to know that. "You have to admit, though, you're bigger than most."

"Well, I appreciate that, darlin'. You know exactly what to say to a man, don't you?" He flicked her nose with the tip of his finger and chuckled when she flushed.

"I didn't mean *that*." She gestured to his general groin area in a circular motion and that only made him laugh harder. "You're such a guy sometimes," she said with a snort of disgust. "I meant, big like tall and…beefy."

"I guess that's better than being doughy or fragile, so I'm going to go out on a limb and take that as a compliment."

"You do that." The sparring between them felt so strange with the addition of this new sexual tension. Like she'd fallen down a rabbit hole or, more likely, into one of the decade's worth of fantasies she had stored up. She crossed the room, waiting for the bathroom door to close so she could breathe again, but felt the heat of his gaze trailing her.

"By the way." His voice had dropped low again, the silky, intimate tone sending her pulse careening. "I like your dress."

"Uh, thanks. I g-got it at Target." Oh, yeah. Very smooth. But still, she couldn't stop the flow. "My mom hates when I shop there. She says it's for poor people."

Perfection. She must have picked up that tidbit in some trendy women's magazine. *If a super-hot guy compliments you, make sure to bring up your mom. And if you can squeeze in a comment about her elitist views, even better.*

To Galen's credit, he only smiled.

"Hurry up and take your shower. I'm starved."

• • •

Half an hour later they were strolling down Los Rosales Street in search of food. It was a good thing, too, because sharing close quarters with him was getting to be an issue. She must have been crazy to agree to spending the next two weeks with him.

"That place looks good," he said, pointing to a terra-cotta building dripping in exotic blooms. The elegant sign above the lanai read FLORES, which was fitting. As they approached, a nattily dressed waiter strode by carrying a heaping plate of lobster, orangey-pink and glistening with butter.

She eyed the tray longingly then gave a regretful shake of her head. "We can't. My dress is too casual for a place like this, and you'd probably need a jacket or at least pants."

"We won't know unless we try. What's the worst thing they can do? Say we can't go in?"

His nonchalance baffled her. It would be mortifying to get turned away. People would probably stare, and the host would think they were a couple of idiots. "I'll pass. The bistro across the street is fine."

He took her wrist and stopped her on the sidewalk. "I thought this was going to be the era of pushing boundaries for you? Now you won't even go to the restaurant where you want to eat? What a chicken."

Her stomach growled at the mention of poultry and Galen sent her a wicked grin. She gnawed on her bottom lip, trying to work up the nerve to go up to the desk, but really, what was the point? They had a lot of time. They could dress appropriately tomorrow and eat there without causing waves. She was all for change, but probably baby steps were better.

"I'd rather go another night," she said primly.

Was it her imagination, or did he look slightly disappointed in her? She refused to explore why the thought bothered her and instead led him toward the bistro.

A few minutes later, they stood by the outdoor bar less than fifty yards from the ocean. The room was long and narrow, with seating designed to take advantage of as much beachfront space as possible. Tables flanked the railing, offering both a breeze and a view, or with a few steps down, patrons could sit at a table in the sand if they chose.

A waitress bustled by with what looked like a mouthwatering plate of shrimp and Lacey grinned. "Nice place."

He nodded. "But don't let the fact that it worked out well this time go to your head. It's always better to take a chance than to be left doing the safe thing and wondering what you're missing. I bet that lobster was fantastic." His tone was teasing but she knew he was only half kidding, just as she knew he was right.

"It's been one day. I'm a work in progress. Don't forget, half of Condado Beach saw my boobs earlier, so I need some recovery time."

She climbed onto a stool, and once she was seated, he did the same. The bartender came over and set menus in front of them. "What can I get you to drink?" he asked with a thick accent. She responded in her high school Spanish, and the waiter grinned.

"What did you order?" Galen asked.

"A *cubre libre* sans the rum."

He chuckled. "So, a Coke?"

"Yeah. With a lime." He clucked his tongue disapprovingly

and she gave him a light shove on the shoulder. "Don't be a bad influence. I may be sitting at the bar, but there is no way I'm drinking after yesterday. Not tonight. In fact, maybe not ever again."

Low, husky laughter met her pronouncement. She and Galen both turned toward the source. A beautiful woman with a pin-straight fall of ebony hair sat a few stools down from them.

"Oh man, I've been there before," the woman said. She was a stunner, with catlike eyes so dark they were almost black. Her sun-kissed skin suggested she'd been in San Juan for a while, although her New England accent indicated that she wasn't a native.

The handsome sandy-haired man with her nodded more enthusiastically than she must have liked, because she gave him a playful swat on the arm. "What?" he protested. "I'm not the one who tells you to mix like that. You're drinking wine, you drink wine. You don't then have a beer and then a mixed drink. Am I right?" This he aimed at Galen, who held up both hands.

"Whoa, no comment. I don't get involved in domestic disputes like this, especially when she's clearly violent."

The couple laughed, and Lacey felt a spurt of envy at Galen's comfort level with strangers. While she'd always been polite, there was a natural banter that his laid-back presence seemed to inspire in spite of his intimidating size. She liked people, but anxiety held her back from making friends very easily. Actually, now that she thought about it, she'd had the same few friends since childhood. Even then it had been the result of another person befriending her, not the other way around.

Cat had instigated their friendship. She'd taken Lacey's Twinkie and pronounced, "We're gonna be bestest friends, you and me." In spite of Lacey's reserved reaction—she was pretty sure she'd shrugged helplessly—deep down, she had been thrilled to bits. Over the moon that this crazy little girl with hair the shade of a new penny, who used her outside voice all the time, would want to be friends with a boring nobody like her.

The man's smooth alto brought her back to the present. "I'm Cyrus, and this is my fiancée, Nikki. So where you guys from?"

"Rhode Island. You?"

"Connecticut."

A long silence ensued, during which Nikki and her man exchanged a glance. "Would you like to join us?" he asked, finally gesturing to the four-top table behind them.

Lacey tamped down the familiar swirl of nervousness and nodded. Dinner with exotic strangers. "That sounds like fun." She couldn't squelch the little rush of delight that swept through her when Galen tipped his head in approval.

At the suggestion of their waiter, she and Cyrus ordered the pork mofongo while Nikki and Galen opted for the catch of the day. Conversation flowed easily, and by the time their meals were served, Lacey felt at ease.

"This is unreal," murmured Galen around a mouthful of grilled red snapper.

He and Lacey ended up passing their plates back and forth for tasting, and Lacey agreed wholeheartedly. The native spices were new to her and sent her senses into overdrive in the best way. She scraped the last remnants of tender roasted meat from her plate and sighed with regret. "Just perfect."

"I tell you, we haven't had a bad meal since we got here," Cyrus said, pushing his almost empty plate away with a groan. "It's only all the walking that's kept me from packing on the pounds."

"Well if that works, I guess that means we can have dessert. Prepare for a marathon tomorrow, Galen."

He turned a lazy, half-lidded gaze toward her. "Dessert? You're going to have to roll me out of here as it is. I haven't eaten like this in eight months."

Cyrus raised a questioning brow.

"Galen is a boxer. He just came off a fight in Atlantic City. It's months of intense training and piles of chicken breast," Lacey confided.

"Ooh, how exciting," Nikki said, eyeing Galen speculatively. "So did you win?"

"He did," Lacey said, pride swelling in her chest. "Knockout in the fifth." It had been a real nail-biter up to that point, and she had spent the majority of the fight pacing in front of the TV. In fact, Marty had snapped at her because she was distracting him from his word puzzle.

"Shit, man, I recognize you now," Cyrus said. "Whalin' Galen Thomas! That's very cool. I don't get the chance to watch too much boxing, but you held the heavyweight belt for a while, didn't you?"

Galen didn't answer, instead raising his brows at Lacey in a clear challenge. She flushed. "He did. From summer of 2009 until mid-2010 when Manny Hermosa stole it in a controversial split decision."

His slow grin melted her insides like butter in the sun. She cleared her throat. "So, uh, hopefully he'll get it back before he retires." Although her gaze was on Cyrus, she could feel Galen's stare.

"I'm impressed," Galen murmured.

"I like boxing," she said, her cheeks burning. "So what do you do for work, Nikki?" she asked, desperately hoping for a change of subject, which Nikki warmed to quickly. She talked about her job in advertising, which she joked was at least as bloody as boxing, but Galen's gaze stayed locked on Lacey, and she struggled to keep from squirming under the weight of it.

Today marked the first time she'd ever admitted that she'd followed his career. Closely. She and Cat had spoken of it in passing, and she'd gone to a couple of the parties the Thomases had hosted on fight nights. Marty had been in the apartment when she'd watched the most recent one, but no one else knew her secret. She hadn't only watched his fights; she'd studied them. In fact, she had an entire collection of DVDs full of every televised matchup he'd ever had.

She always figured, if anyone found out, she could rationalize it with a response like, *Hey, if you went to high school with Britney Spears, you'd buy her albums.* But that wasn't it at all. It was an opportunity to watch him in his element without him seeing the truth on her face.

She was crazy about him.

"What about you, Lacey?" Nikki asked.

"I work for my family's law firm as the marketing director."

"Wow, big job. Do you enjoy it?"

She opened her mouth to give her standard affirmative reply but stopped short. Did she enjoy it? She considered the question carefully. More than some things. Like jury duty and going to the gynecologist. But it wasn't as much fun as, say, karaoke or taking in an action flick on a rainy Saturday afternoon. That's what a job was, though, right? It wasn't called happy fun play time. It was called work.

"It's fine, as jobs go," she hedged. "It was a given that I would join the firm, and I really don't have the heart for criminal law, so it seemed like a good compromise."

Cyrus nodded. "That's how I feel. I work in finance, and it pays the bills, but it's nothing to write home about. My free time is when I loosen up and enjoy life." He leaned closer to his bride-to-be and squeezed her thigh. "Speaking of which, I know you said you're never drinking again, but we have mojito makings and an awesome patio back at our place. Hot tub, pool, the whole nine. It's a gorgeous night, so why don't you guys come with us and hang out a while? It's only half a mile down the beach. We can walk off some of this food."

His gaze lingered on Lacey for a long moment, and she got a weird whiff of attraction coming from him. Surely she was mistaken. A handsome guy like Cyrus with a beautiful fiancée like Nikki wouldn't be checking out a seven like Lacey, would he? The moment passed so quickly, she was sure she'd imagined it.

"What do you think?" Galen asked.

She shrugged. It was a beautiful night, and she didn't relish the thought of going back to their villa yet. Better to keep busy rather than stew over her wedding day debacle.

"Well, I guess I could have one mojito, but then definitely no dessert," Lacey said.

"You guys get the check while me and Lacey powder our noses," Nikki said, before planting a smacking kiss on Cyrus's cheek.

Lacey hesitated. The other couple had assumed she and Galen were an item, and it had seemed less important to correct them than it had to avoid putting a label on what they were, so neither of them had objected. Now, though, sticking Galen with the check felt crummy. He noted her hesitation and made an *are you kidding me* face, shooing her away with a wave of his hand. Both of them were comfortable financially, and a meal certainly wasn't going to break the bank. She vowed to pick up the next one and trailed behind Nikki to the ladies room.

"I'm so glad we met. We still have another week, and

as much as I love being with Cyrus, all this one-on-one togetherness was driving us both a little mad," Nikki confided as she rifled through her bright green crocheted bag. "I confess, an hour into meeting you guys, I was fantasizing about tearing you away from that hunk of yours so we could engage in some retail therapy. Maybe mani pedis?"

Lacey wasn't sure how to respond. It sounded like fun, but could she really go hang out with someone she'd just met? What if Nikki spent an hour with her and realized how dorky she was and regretted it? Or maybe she was like Cat and would appreciate having a dorky friend. Still, she hesitated.

Nikki held up a hand. "No pressure. Just, after a few days, you might be bored, too, you know?"

Lacey wanted to reassure her, but what could she say without sounding like a lame ass? *I'd love to go shopping with you but, boo hoo, I don't make friends very easily so this is weird for me.* No, that would be the old Lacey who hung around guys like Marty. She was with Galen. Well, maybe not *with* him, with him, but...

She opted to play it cool. "Yeah, I totally agree on the too-much-one-on-one-togetherness thing. Major snoozeville. I'm definitely up for shopping at some point, so count me in."

Nikki flashed a big grin. "Fab." She went to dab some coral gloss onto her lips but hesitated. Eyeing Lacey in the mirror, she said, "I kinda had a feeling about you. About the two of you."

Lacey tried not to fidget under her intense stare. Great. She already suspected that she and Galen weren't a couple. It shouldn't bother her. Heck, anyone could see they were a mismatch. She didn't have any illusions about herself. She was reasonably attractive but Galen? Galen was sex on a plate, extra spicy. Now that the jig was up, there was no point in pretending, but it stung a little. "Obvious, huh?"

Nikki smiled and popped her brows. "I had a hunch. Full swap?" She held the pot of her lip gloss aloft.

Lacey eyed the gloss in Nikki's hand, then down at her own and shrugged. What the hell? The color would look great with her dress, and new Lacey wouldn't even *think* about the germs. "Sure." She handed over her pink passion and plucked the coral color from Nikki's fingers.

"Cool." Nikki grinned and dabbed some of Lacey's gloss onto her full lips. "Ready?"

Lacey applied the other woman's gloss and nodded with relief. "Yep."

"Ooh, that color looks super sexy on you! You can keep it." She gave Lacey a broad wink and Lacey winked back. Seemed like Nikki wasn't going to press for details about her and Galen's relationship, which was fine by her.

Nikki snapped her purse closed and linked her arm through Lacey's. "Let's go get 'em."

She was so...so hip and seemed so together that even if it was for a couple short weeks, why couldn't Lacey pretend she was one of the cool crowd? The past twenty-four hours had been filled with bikinis, worldly new friends, and the risk of herpes simplex B. If that wasn't living on the edge, she didn't know what was. Why, if Cat were there, she would've been cheering her on with two-fingered whistles and foot stomps.

She donned the most go-with-the-flow, cool expression she could muster and nodded. "Yeah, let's skedaddle."

• • •

Lacey Garrity had watched all of his fights. Not just watched, judging by her in-depth recollections, but studied. It humbled him, and he was buoyed by the revelation. He didn't want to read into it too much, but maybe she'd been harboring a little crush on him at some point that had gotten her interested in his boxing. When they were younger, a few times he'd caught her looking at him when she thought he didn't see, but he'd taken it as nothing more than girlish curiosity in the physique of a growing boy. Now he wondered if it had been more than that, and what things might have been like for them if he'd known sooner and had acted on it. Maybe she never would've married that asshole Marty, and they could've had a shot at something. But that ship had sailed.

Hadn't it? He was still mulling that over when the ladies emerged from the bathroom. Nikki was chuckling, and Lacey looked happy and relaxed. He marveled that, in such a short time, she was already so much more at ease than he'd ever seen her. He had to admit, it looked good on her. Their day at the beach gave her skin a warm glow, and he resisted the urge to trace the delicate line of her shoulder.

"Ready?" she asked with a smile.

The four of them filed out of the restaurant and headed by tacit agreement toward the beach. The sun had plummeted off the horizon when the palm trees started to sing. *Co-kee, co-kee*.

"What is that?" Lacey whispered.

"Coquí frogs," Nikki said. "Isn't it lovely?"

"So neat. Do they do it every night?"

"Every night we've been here."

They fell into a companionable silence as they strolled along the shore. With the waves lapping against the sand and the coquí singing their song, it seemed like the most natural thing in the world to take Lacey's hand. She stiffened and looked his way, but a second later, her fingers curled around his. It felt nice. More than nice. It felt…strangely right. The thought unsettled him. The last thing he needed was to get too emotionally attached. If things weren't so complicated for her, it would be one thing, but falling in love with a neurotic woman who just got jilted at the altar and only wanted a rebound guy? That was a recipe for pain. Not going to happen. When she was ready, he would be happy to offer his body for her as-yet-untapped bad girl to practice on, but he was going to keep both hands up and protect his heart.

Cyrus and Nikki pulled ahead a bit, but Lacey seemed content to stroll, so he didn't increase his pace. Their actions certainly weren't doing anything to dissuade their new friends from thinking the two of them were a couple, but that didn't bother him in the least. In fact, maybe now was a good time to see if that bad girl was ready to come out and play. He tugged her to a stop and bent low to pick up a flat stone.

"The water's pretty calm. Know how to skip?"

She laughed. "Well, duh. Your sister is my best friend. You think the undisputed champion of Pawtucket Lake would allow me to go through life without learning how to skip a rock?" She dropped his hand and began searching the sand for a suitable stone. "A-ha!" She squatted down and came up with two perfect specimens. "Ready? I'll bet I can get more hops than you."

He snorted. "First off, 'undisputed' is entirely inaccurate. I dispute the shit out of Cat's claim. Second, you're on. I'll even make it easy for you. My one to your two."

They made their way to the water's edge. "I know your stance on the whole 'ladies first' thing, so why don't you go ahead."

He chuckled and stepped up. "Watch and learn." Waiting a beat until the gentle incoming wave crashed, he flicked his wrist and sent his stone skimming across the surface. One, two, three, four skips.

Lacey let out a low whistle. "Not bad. Now me." She took a deep breath and blew it out before snapping her arm out to send the rock skittering across the water. One, two, three, four, five…shit.

"Seven! Woo-hoo! I am the champion!" she crowed, pumping her fist.

He laughed and shook his head. "One win doesn't make you the champ, squirt."

She stuck a hand on her hip and cocked her head to the side. "Why not? You beat Mickey Lewis one time and became champ. In fact, I think I deserve a belt."

"I'll give you a belt all right," he said with a grin. But when her words sank in, he stepped closer. "Speaking of that, I'm happy to hear that you watch my fights, Lacey."

He stepped closer, brushing a lock of hair from her cheek, and her breath caught. When her body swayed toward his, he leaned in. "Picturing you, in front of your TV, rooting me on? It makes me feel real good, and I can't quite put my finger on why. But I know that I like it."

The air seemed thin suddenly, and their harsh breathing eclipsed the sound of the waves. They stood, frozen for a long moment, until she tipped her head up, almost imperceptibly. He swallowed hard and bent low, his lips just touching the softness of hers, and her arms slipped around his hips—

"You guys coming or what?"

Cyrus's voice calling from ahead dragged him back to reality with a jolt and he reluctantly pulled away. Lacey's lashes fluttered and she shook her head.

"W-we shouldn't do that anyway." She sucked in a ragged breath. "Or anything else. Probably."

He pursed his lips together to keep from smiling. "Okay. Then you might want to get your hand off my ass."

She snatched it away like he was on fire and took a leaping step back. "Right. Sorry. I want to…kiss you. But I'm married."

Hearing those words come out of her mouth sent an irrational spurt of jealousy coursing through his veins. "Semantics," he said. "You won't be soon, and considering the circumstances, surely you don't feel like you're bound to those promises."

"I don't know how I feel." She bit her lip and slowly shook her head. "Yesterday morning I was a newlywed. Today I'm a separated, soon-to-be divorcée, and I'm not really sure how to be that."

"You need to learn to live for *you* and do what you want to do." He brushed the hair from her face. "We're here together now. In thirteen days, it's back to life. I, for one, would love to spend those thirteen days with you. Touching you. Kissing you. Showing you all the things Marty couldn't."

Her face crumpled, and he swore under his breath. He'd pushed too hard. Just because it was obvious to him that she didn't owe Marty a damned thing didn't mean it was obvious to her. If and when she realized that, and recognized that she wasn't suffering from a broken heart, but from a bruised ego, he'd be there, ready to blow her mind. The thought of teaching her about the pleasure her body was capable of made him ache. He pulled away. "You're right. Let's take a step back here. I want you to know that I'm here. For whatever you need."

"Thanks," she said softly.

"Hello-o-o?" Nikki yelled.

He took her hand and they jogged toward the other couple. "Sorry, we're right behind you," he called.

A little ways farther down the beach, Cyrus stopped in front of a sprawling villa made of white sandstone.

"This is you?" Lacey asked with a nod to the house.

"This is us." Nikki grinned. "Pretty nice, right? Cyrus's boss owns it and offered it up for the whole month after Cyrus closed a huge deal for them."

"Nice," Lacey agreed.

Cyrus unlocked a whitewashed wooden gate and they stepped into what looked like a miniature rain forest. Calling this setup a patio was the understatement of the millennium. It was an oasis. A slice straight out of *The Blue Lagoon*. The pool, which was illuminated from within by ethereal lights, was the irregular shape of a natural spring, encased in ochre-colored stone. A waterfall flanked by towering palms flowed over a shelf of heather gray boulders.

"Wow." Lacey gasped. "Our villa has a little pool, but nothing like this. It's breathtaking."

"I know, right?" Nikki chuckled. "It'll be hard going back home after this. You guys can get in or hang while Cy and I make some drinks."

The couple went into the house, leaving him alone with Lacey.

She shook her head in amazement. "This place is ridiculous. I've never seen anything like it."

"Let's go in then," he said.

"I don't have a suit on under this, and I don't want to borrow one from Nikki. I already shared lip gloss with her," she confided. "It was in a little pot and I used my finger, though. You think that's okay?" she whispered, shooting a glance to the patio doors to make sure their hosts didn't hear.

"What do you mean, okay?" he whispered back, trying not to grin.

"I mean, I'm not going to get mono or something, am I? All this spontaneity is a little scary, if you ask me."

"I'm thinking you're probably okay on the mono thing. As for a swimsuit, a bra and underwear is no more revealing than a bikini," Galen reasoned. "And we've already established that you've gone skinny-dipping, not to mention you flashing half of San Juan this morning. This should be a cinch."

She groaned and covered her cheeks with her hands. "What are the odds of my living that down anytime soon?"

"Very slim. Now come on. We'll hop in before they come out and they won't see. I'll even turn my back." He did so and waited. A long, silent moment passed. "Well?"

"I'm scared," she mumbled.

"We're never going to be in this spot again. I don't want to leave and for you to have regrets about the things you didn't do while we were here. Besides, there's nothing to be afraid of. I would never let anything happen to you. If I did, Cat would kill me," he added hastily in case she confused his declaration of loyalty with something more.

She blew out a sigh. "You're right." The determination in her voice gave him hope and he waited. His patience was rewarded as the sound of rustling clothes came from behind him. He unbuttoned his own shirt and tossed it onto a lounge chair.

"Ready?"

"I'm getting in first, so don't turn around yet."

A light splash of water, a sharp hiss of breath. The instinct to turn around was so strong he fisted his hands at his sides and silently counted in Spanish. It took concentration, since his Spanish was only slightly better than his needlepoint, and he'd only gotten to *seis* when she called to him.

"Okay, ready."

When he turned, Lacey waded toward him in the lagoon-like pool, long wet hair spread around her bare shoulders, looking like a water nymph from a fairy tale.

"Come on, it's nice and warm."

Oh, man, he bet it was. She dove to the side, breaking through the water with a splash. If an iridescent scaled tail had trailed behind her, it wouldn't have seemed out of place.

"She's a stone cold fox," Cyrus said as he stepped onto the porch with a tray of drinks in hand.

"You're not kidding." Nikki stopped short behind her fiancé and added a low whistle for good measure.

"Thanks," he said, not really sure how else to respond. It was a weird spot to be in because she wasn't his girlfriend, but they didn't know that. And, judging by the way they were both looking at her, it seemed prudent to keep it that way.

Cyrus handed him a drink. "You can take it in. There's a bar in the center of the water about halfway down, past the waterfall, where you can set it before the water gets too deep to stand. You go ahead. Nikki and I are going to get some towels and put on some music."

"Thanks." He took a sip of the tart drink and padded to the water's edge. It didn't drop off like a regular backyard swimming pool. Rather, it sloped downward like a beach. He walked down the gentle incline until he was up to his waist.

"Are you in yet?" Lacey called. "You *have* to see this!"

Her voice seemed to echo from an outcropping of rocks she had disappeared around. Maybe nymph was the wrong mythical creature. Siren was more like it. He made his way toward the sound of her delighted voice, his pulse gunning like an outboard motor.

The waterfall's applause must have drowned out his arrival because she startled when he came around the corner. Then she saw him, and her face stretched into a smile.

"Look."

She led him toward what looked like a tiny pond inside the pool, set apart by a tidy row of stones. In the incandescent light, boldly colored fish swam around in lazy circles, gold, orange, and red. When he moved closer, a few darted away, taking cover under the creamy water lilies that dotted the surface.

When he turned to Lacey, he recognized her expression. She wanted to gauge his reaction. He knew the need to be the person who introduced someone else to something amazing. The phenomenon was one reserved for people whose opinions really mattered. The idea that Lacey wanted to impress him gave him a bone-deep satisfaction, because he sure as shit wanted to impress her. Show her new things. Blow her mind.

His cock twitched, and he struggled to keep his eyes on the fish. No way he wanted to backslide again like they had on the beach, not when they were just gaining ground.

"Cool, right?" Lacey pressed.

"Very. I've always wanted a koi pond, but this is over the top."

"It's the most amazing thing I've ever seen. I don't care what I have to do, but some day I'm getting one of these."

She looked so happy, so fucking hopeful at that moment, he wished he had a camera. Something about a happy, hopeful Lacey made him feel damned good inside.

He handed her the drink. "Want some?"

"Yeah." She turned full around to face him. Her nude bra was plastered to her like a second skin, but it had stayed fairly opaque. He must have made a sound, some indication of his disappointment, because she frowned.

"You okay?"

"Yep. Fine," he lied.

She took the drink and sipped delicately. "Oh, yum. I could so get used to this place."

"Are you glad we came?"

"To Puerto Rico or to Cyrus and Nikki's?"

"Both. Either."

She tipped her head to the side and regarded him for a long moment before nodding. "Yeah, I am. When I get back home, I'm going to try to do things differently. You were right about regrets. I think I'm sick of missing out."

"Are you?" He hadn't meant the words to sound loaded, but there they were. Dripping with challenge, ripe with questions.

"Yes. From now on, I'm taking every opportunity to try new th—" She paused and her eyes went wide. "Wait, th-that's not the same thing," she said, but her voice was so low, he wasn't sure whether she was trying to convince him or herself, so he stayed silent. "I want to. You have no idea how much I want to," she added with a short laugh. "But there'd be something hanging over it. Something ugly. And after all the times I've thought of—" She took a gulp of mojito, then turned her bourbon-colored eyes on him. "How about a compromise? One kiss, here under the waterfall, so I can remember this exact place and moment of freedom with you. No regrets."

His mind was racing faster than Usain Bolt at the Olympics. He was so caught up with the *After all the times I've thought of* part, he almost missed the invitation. Almost.

He plucked the drink from her fingers and set it on a flat rock, then took her hand. He didn't speak as they made their way toward the waterfall, afraid to break the spell. When they reached the shelf of rocks beneath the rushing water, he turned and put his hands on her waist. "Ready?"

She nodded, her eyes wide, and he stepped under the spray, pulling her in with him. For a second, they were pummeled with a hard blast, but then it was gone, and they were behind the wall of water, tucked into the hidden space behind the waterfall.

In spite of her obvious nerves, she stepped closer, bridging the gap between them until they touched. "This is for watching my fights and rooting for me," he murmured, pressing a soft kiss to her forehead. "And this is for being brave and accepting my dare." He pressed a second kiss on the tip of her nose. "And this is for dumping that dickhead Marty." The next kiss landed on the corner of her mouth, and she parted her lips on a sigh. His heart hammered so loudly, he wondered if she heard it.

"And this one? This one is because I want you so bad, it's making me question my sanity." He tipped his head low as blood rushed to his ears, the grind of need demanding that he slant his mouth over hers and take and take and take. But when his lips touched hers, he was consumed by an even stronger desire to sip and nip and taste. He traced her plump bottom lip with the tip of his tongue, then sank his teeth softly into the tender flesh.

"Oh, my," she whispered.

He breathed in her gasp and smiled against her mouth. "Oh your what?"

"That's nice." She shimmied closer to him, wedging herself between the *V* of his thighs, smashing her soft breasts against his chest. "Again," she demanded.

He groaned and dove in for more. She wrapped her slim arms around his waist and clung to him, sliding her tongue against his, whimpering low in her throat. She sucked at his bottom lip, each pull of her mouth sending a pulse of pleasure through him. Her mouth was liquid fire, sweet and tart from the drink, and it took all of his will not to consume her. Take complete control of the kiss and more. So much more…

Only a kiss.

She nipped him then, sweeping her tongue over the sensitive flesh on the inside of his bottom lip. Her boldness sent blood rushing to his cock and he tipped his hips closer, trying to ease the ache. She responded with a moan of approval, grinding her pelvic bone against him in the most erotic of dances. Her breasts heaved against his chest, the softness beckoning him. He trailed his fingers from the soft curve of hip over the dip of her waist and traced her rib cage. The pulsing of her hips against him grew faster, harder as his thumb traced patterns right where her bra met skin.

"Please," she murmured against his mouth.

Goddammit, this was only supposed to be a kiss, his conscience bellowed. But as he pulled back and saw the naked hunger on her face, he could no more deny her at that moment than he could sprout wings and fly away.

He held her gaze as he slipped his index finger beneath her bra strap and slid it slowly down her shoulder. The upper swell of her breast came into view, inch by glorious inch, until the wet fabric caught on her tight little nipple. His cock bucked against his boxers, and he groaned.

"One taste," he promised, not sure whether he was trying to convince her or himself.

He bent low as he flipped the last bit of satin away from the dusky peak. First, a close-mouthed kiss. Then, the flick of his tongue. She stiffened in his arms.

"Oh my God," she whimpered.

She trembled against him, and he closed his lips over her, rubbing his tongue against the sensitive bud until she was muttering incoherently, her fingers digging into his scalp, urging him to keep going. The need to obey her unwitting and sensual command, to make her come until her throat was sore from screaming his name, battered him like the waves from a monsoon. Sweat broke out on his upper lip and he trembled with the effort of restraining himself.

Then she moaned low in her throat, a wordless plea, and he couldn't deny her. Just a little more… He trailed his fingers over the thin fabric of her tiny panties, sliding beneath to cup her heat in his hand. She froze, then cried out, the sound echoing against the rocks. He slid his finger into her wet center, and she closed around him like liquid silk. He wasted no time, and began to fuck her with his finger. In and out he slid until she bore down against him, trying to take him deeper. His heart jackhammered against his ribs, and a growl reverberated in his chest. Using the edge of his teeth, he tugged on her nipple and slid his finger deeper.

"Please, Galen, I—" She whimpered, clutching fistfuls of his hair in her hands.

Her hips fluttered now, moving counterpoint to his thrusts. His name was a litany on her lips and her body tensed, straining against him. She was close. God, she was so fucking close. And his cock was loaded for bear and he was a suck, fuck, or jerk away from the point of no return.

The last working part of his brain sent up a warning flare. They should stop. But, damn, she was so ready...

As if she could hear his thoughts, she froze. "I-I can't do this. I'm not ready yet."

He wanted to howl with disappointment, but he knew she was right. She'd feel guilty if they finished this, regardless of the fact that she had nothing to feel guilty for. And no matter what her body was telling him, he didn't want to be responsible for her regret. Reluctantly, he pulled his hand away, slipping her panties back in place and releasing her nipple with a muttered curse. "You're right. We should get back anyway."

Their harsh breaths mingled in the warm night air and she nodded, looking dazed. She blinked up at him and disentangled her hand from his hair. She swallowed hard, her throat working. "I guess we *were* being rude."

He held her gaze and traced his finger over the delicate line of her collarbone and adjusted her bra. "I, for one, couldn't give a shit about being rude if it meant we could pick up where we stopped, but I don't want you doing anything you'll regret. This isn't over, though. Something's going on here and we're going to need to figure out what to do about it eventually." He let his gaze slide down her front to where her nipples still pressed taut against wet satin. "I have several suggestions if you want to hear them."

Despite the heat in her eyes at his words, she shook her head vigorously. "Nope. That's a bad idea." She scrambled backward and then pitched forward into the water. A moment later she was wading toward the patio in a graceless, splashy breaststroke, a frantic attempt to get some distance from him before calling back over her shoulder. "But feel free to write down those thoughts and share them with me after my—"

"Look out!"

His warning came too late as she promptly smacked her head against a decorative stone.

"Son of a—" she mumbled under her breath. To her credit, she barely paused, navigating around the rock and propelling herself forward with a one-armed crawl. "It's fine," she called over her shoulder. "Seriously. All good. Barely nicked me. See you back at the patio."

He winced, although part of him was glad to see some proof that she was as affected by what had happened between them as he was. He gave her a minute to collect herself, another so he could do the same, then followed her. He'd just rounded the bend when he saw Lacey standing in the middle of the pool, frozen to the spot with a bare-assed Cyrus next to her, his arm around her shoulder.

"So," Nikki said, wading toward Galen. "Did you guys want to do this all together, or are we going our separate ways?" She stood when she reached him, bare breasts bobbing on the surface like buoys.

Cyrus turned to face them and Galen quickly averted his gaze, but not before he got an eyeful of Cyrus's one-eyed Willy, locked and loaded for action.

"We're down with either one," Cyrus said with an affable smile. The call of the coquí frogs seemed to grow louder in the heavy silence.

Galen turned the evidence this way and that, trying to make sense of the scene. But after an endless moment, he knew there was only one plausible explanation.

Their hip new friends were swingers, and they wanted to do the old swap-around with Lacey and him.

Well, shit.

Chapter Six

Blood rushed to Lacey's ears and her brain froze. Cyrus's lips were moving, but his words weren't making any sense. *We're down with either one.*

She opened her mouth and then closed it again with a snap, unable to fully grasp what was happening. Cyrus's fingers traced a path from her shoulder to the nape of her neck, and although she didn't feel any malice coming from him, the desire to jerk away was almost overpowering.

Galen locked gazes with her and gave her a reassuring smile. There was no tension in his tone when he turned to Nikki and spoke. "Listen, I'm flattered, and I'm sure Lacey is, too, but—"

"Ah, the 'but.'" The other man's grin turned sheepish as he released Lacey and stepped away. "I'm really sorry; I thought this was already sort of agreed upon." He sent his fiancée an irritated look. "I told you, babe. They've only got eyes for each other. You were way off."

Nikki's brow wrinkled and she ran a hand through her wet hair. "When we were in the ladies room at the restaurant, I out and out asked her if she would do a full switch and she said yeah…"

Lacey's face burned. "I thought you meant the lip gloss." She crossed her arms over her chest, suddenly feeling more naked than she'd felt when the tide had swept away her bikini top.

Nikki chuckled, and then her chuckles turned into full belly laughter. A moment later, Cyrus joined her. "Oh my God." She gasped, swiping tears from her eyes with her knuckle. "I had no clue what you were doing with that. Cy, she sort of took my lip gloss and gave me hers and I was totally baffled, thinking, *Must be a Rhode Island thing.*"

Cyrus howled and Galen's ear-to-ear grin made Lacey's cheeks burn even more. Still, they were handling it really well, and when she thought about it, it was kind of funny.

"It must have been wishful thinking on my part," Nikki said, setting a hungry gaze on Galen. Just when a stab of jealousy poked through Lacey's semi-shock, Nikki set an equally hungry gaze on Lacey. "I don't know who's sexier, him or you."

"Definitely him," Lacey blurted.

That got them laughing again, although it took Lacey a little while to catch up.

When the chuckles died down, there was a long and uncomfortable silence. "So are we all cool then? Friends but not luvahs? Unless of course you change your mind," Nikki said, waggling her brows.

Could these cool, beautiful people actually be attracted to her? Boring, white-bread Lacey? In spite of her embarrassment, she found herself just a little tickled at the thought. Instead of hiding her flaming-hot face like she wanted to, Lacey smiled. "Sure thing."

They all stood around, unsure of what to do next, when Galen saved the day. "On that note, I think it's probably best if we call it a night. Neither of us got a whole lot of sleep and we still have to walk back. We truly appreciate your hospitality."

Galen inched toward the side of the pool, waiting for her to follow suit. She sent a panicked glance at Cyrus and Nikki, who took pity on her by swimming off deeper into the lagoon. As soon as they were out of sight, she scurried out of the pool and into the towel Galen held out for her.

"You okay to walk back or do you want to get a cab?" he asked softly.

"It's less than a mile; we can walk." Despite the balmy air, her lips were trembling and she pressed them together to make them stop.

"It's okay, squirt. You're okay. We had a great night until that weirdness at the end, and you handled yourself beautifully. Now let's get the hell out of here before they think we changed our minds." That got her moving and a few minutes later, they were dressed and calling out their good-byes to Cyrus and Nikki.

They headed off back down the beach toward the villa. To his credit, Galen didn't say a negative word to her. The old Galen would have. He would have raked her over the coals about her naiveté and busted her chops mercilessly about the whole incident. *Lip gloss, indeed.* Her cheeks warmed again and she broke the silence with a groan. "Oh my God, that was so mortifying." She had opened the floodgates, so surely now he would tease her about it.

Instead, he shrugged. "No biggie."

No biggie? She'd weathered her first—and hopefully last—orgy invitation, and he said, "No biggie"? She spared a glance his way, wishing she could see his expression better in the dim light. Was he disappointed? Wishing she'd agreed so he could get some one-on-one time with Nikki? The thought didn't sit well. "I know you said you didn't want me to have any regrets or miss out on any experiences, but I hope you understand why I couldn't do…that."

It took so long for him to reply, she started to wonder if he even heard her. Then, a few short steps from their villa door, he tugged her to a stop. "For someone as smart as you, your instincts sure suck."

"What do you mean?"

"I mean there is no way I'd want you to be with someone else, especially not in front of me. But let's get one thing straight, squirt. When you come to your senses and you're ready to have the experience of a lifetime? I'm your guy. I'm the one you're going to get wild with." He took her wrist and tugged her close until they were pressed together. Thighs against thighs. Hips against hips. "I'm the one who's going to show you that getting down and dirty doesn't mean rolling in the wet sand."

The past two days had been the craziest of her life, and she didn't know how much longer she could hold up against the battering ram of his sexual attention. Their carnal kiss and head-to-toe embrace was tattooed on her brain, a live-action trailer of what could be if she stopped being such a prude. She had been *right there*, but for stupid Marty hanging over her head. Even now, she felt tense, like her skin was on too tight. As if her body knew that she'd left the only orgasm of her life back at that pool and was rebelling against her for pulling away. Her muscles clenched under the intensity of his gaze, but before she could stammer a response, he stepped back.

"But not until you're ready." He took out their key and opened the door.

Relief warred with disappointment. He was letting her off the hook. For now. He waved her through the door, following close behind.

"That was a pretty interesting way to spend an evening,"

he said, his tone light as he closed the door behind them.

"Interesting is putting it mildly," she said, happy to take the reprieve. "Cat's not going to believe this. My first orgy. That's even crazier than the time she and that fireman—"

He clapped his hands over his ears. "Jesus Christ, Lacey, I don't want to hear that shit. I'm going to have to bleach my brain. And anyway, it wasn't exactly an orgy. More like a near miss." She frowned and he uncovered his ear. "It doesn't make it any less awesome, though," he assured her. "It's an honor just to be nominated."

Surely this was the most absurd conversation ever. She'd expected to be a married woman, exploring Old San Juan with her husband Marty all day today…or at least until his sciatica started acting up. Instead, she was here talking about her almost-orgy after nearly having sex in the pool with Galen. Her nemesis. Her tormentor. Her dream guy. The dream guy who had rocked her straight down to her toes less than an hour ago. Strange how life threw curveballs like that out of nowhere.

"You want some iced tea?" he asked, making his way to the kitchen.

"No, thanks." She padded across the marble floor and sat on the edge of the couch, pressing her fingers to her lips. Here he was, casually talking about iced tea, and all she could think of was his mouth. How was she going to get it out of her mind now that she'd tasted it?

And his hands…God, those hands.

Hands that don't belong on you, she reminded herself. No matter how much she wished otherwise, she was still a married woman, and what they'd done was wrong.

It didn't feel wrong.

Suddenly, the adrenaline of the night drained from her body, and her rioting emotions came to a dead halt. The ensuing numbness was almost a relief. No more thinking for the night. She was like a dog chasing its tail and getting nowhere anyway. Once she got a good night's sleep, she'd sit down and figure out how to handle this, and more importantly, how to handle Galen.

She flopped to the side and curled up her legs. Briefly, she contemplated changing out of her damp bra and underwear and into her pajamas but then dismissed it. A few minutes of rest first. She couldn't hold back the loud, hippo-like yawn. "I think the last couple days are catching up with me, because I totally just hit the wall."

"Just change and go to bed, then. Once I get out of these clothes, I'm going to get some shut-eye myself."

She grumbled and shifted, settling more deeply into the cushions. "You go ahead, and by the time you're done I'll be ready to get up." Maybe she'd close her eyes for a few minutes until he returned. Being wild was exhausting.

. . .

Soft snores greeted him as he reentered the living room. He shook his head, bemused. Lacey was the only person he knew who could fall asleep in less than a minute. Didn't matter where it was, either, or what was happening around her. She'd gone on a camping trip with his family the year she and Cat were starting high school. He was going into junior year and couldn't believe his parents hadn't let him stay home alone. Then they'd made it ten times worse by letting Cat bring a friend. He was going to be stuck in the woods for seven days with Tweedle-Annoying and Tweedle-Even-More-Annoying. Awesome.

Up to that point, he'd made it his life's work to mess with them both, but at fifteen, even that was beneath him.

In preparation for the coming school year, he'd taken to aggressively ignoring them. Cleary, that wasn't going to work for this camping trip, because the three of them—Cat, Lacey, and him—had been unceremoniously smashed into the backseat of his mother's Civic. Lacey had gotten the hump in the center because she was the smallest, but that left her pressed up against his side like some kind of person-sized parasite, sucking his perpetual horniness to the surface. Beanpole or not, she was still a teenage girl, and he was a mass of hormones writhing under the paper-thin wrappings of a teenage boy. While he sat and suffered, two minutes into the trip—yes, before they'd even left city limits—she was snoring, with her face pressed against his shoulder.

For four hours, she tortured him. Her leg, bared to the thigh in her white cotton shorts, rubbing against his with every turn. Her nearly nonexistent breasts jiggling, just a little, every time his father hit a pothole. Her hand, flopping to his lap, so close to the mother lode he was reduced to gritting his teeth. And on she slept, like a rock, sawing wood as if she didn't have a care in the world. A teenage sleeping Lacey. While the boy in him had found her hard to resist back then, in spite of his every effort to hide it, the man in him now was in far worse shape.

The memory had him grinning like an idiot as he stared down at grown-up sleeping Lacey. Now he was in a jam, though, because he wasn't sure if he should bring her into the bedroom for a comfortable night's sleep or if he should leave her on the couch. That morning, they'd called and asked for extra bedding from the concierge and had set up the small spare room for him to sleep in, so it was easy to take his own feelings out of it. Sharing a bed with her again wasn't an option.

A puff of cool air from the vent above hit him on the back

of the neck and it was settled. She was still in damp clothes and the room was chilly. She really needed to change. He knelt beside her and shook her shoulder gently. "Lacey, wake up."

"Go 'way," she mumbled before flipping onto her side with a snuffle.

He grinned and tried again, shaking a little harder. *Nada.* With a sigh, he bent low and scooped her up. Immediately, her arms circled his neck and she pressed closer. He steeled himself and crossed the room, trying to ignore the softness of her breast branding his chest as he walked. Jesus, maybe it was because his body was still in hyperdrive from their petting in the pool, but by the time they reached one of the bedrooms, he was sporting a full-blown hard-on.

Not bothering to flick on the light, he set her gently on the bed. He tried to disengage himself, but she would have none of it. She kept her arms locked around his neck and yanked until he was sprawled on top of her.

"Don't wanna be alone," she murmured, burying her nose into his throat. He rolled to the side, tugging her along with him until she lay in the crook of his arm. With a contented sigh, she snuggled in deeper and hooked her thigh over his hip. Hot blood roared to his cock. What the fuck was he going to do now? Over the past two days, he'd seen a side of Lacey he'd never seen before and, if he was being totally honest with himself, he'd thought she was pretty great before. Now he knew that, on top of her kind-hearted if not somewhat neurotic nature and smoking-hot body, she'd also been hiding a well of untapped sensuality. It was a lethal combination. He couldn't remember ever wanting to touch someone so badly he could taste it.

She'd made herself clear, though. She wasn't about to go there with him. Not right now, anyway. And maybe now was all they had. Maybe this was a fluke, an anomaly created by the perfect storm of events that would subside once they left the island. Then they'd go back to their regularly scheduled program. A program that didn't include him wanting to tear off her clothes and make her scream his name over and over.

Then again, maybe this was always the way it was meant to go. Maybe the timing had never been right. There had been a short period in grade school where he thought she might have a crush on him, but he'd been far too old for her. When they finally bridged the perceived gap, they were in high school. He was way too cool to hang out with his little sister and her friends, and she certainly hadn't seemed interested anyway. By the time they reached adulthood, one of them always seemed to have a significant other and it had been so easy to fall into the sniping that had become the norm for them. But now, he was single and she was well on her way to the same. Maybe this was their time.

Whenever she's ready, he reminded himself.

He inched away, trying to get a little space between them, but for every centimeter he gained, she scooted two closer until she was almost on top of him. Her warm breath tickled his neck and he grudgingly gave up the fight as the lure of a warm female on a comfortable bed after a long day of sun and surf took over.

He slid his hand into her hair and closed his eyes, letting the image of her in her bikini bottoms, bare breasts streaked with sand, play like a silent film against the backs of his eyelids. His cock throbbed against her thigh and he groaned. Thirteen nights left.

Which was unfortunate, because at this rate? He'd be dead in three.

Chapter Seven

"Unless something's changed, I'm going to have to ask that you unhand me."

Galen's sleep-roughened voice poured over her like honey, and her eyes drifted opened. His handsome face, made even more so by the morning whiskers shadowing his jaw, came into focus. "What do you mean?"

He flipped his heavy-lidded gaze downward, and she followed suit.

"Omigod. I am so sorry!" She jerked her hand away and covered her mouth in mortification. For the second morning in a row, one of her appendages had wound up in up-close-and-personal contact with his manly parts.

"Hey, no harm no foul. I'm not usually one to complain about waking up to a morning cock massage, but I didn't want to reach the boiling point only to find out you were actually dead asleep and dreaming about milking a cow."

She closed her eyes and ducked her head under the covers, wishing she could disappear. "How did we end up in the same bed again?" She remembered falling asleep on the couch, but after that, it was all a pleasant blur.

"Cut it out." His muffled voice became clear as he yanked the blanket off her head. "I can't even hear you like that."

She picked a spot on the wall and stared at it, hard. "I asked how we got in the same bed again."

"I put you in and you didn't want to be alone." He shrugged. "Far be it from me to argue with a pretty lady. And frankly, until about ten seconds ago, I was thinking it was a great decision out of me."

Despite the teasing words, she could feel the sexual tension rolling off him. It took all her strength not to bolt before she jumped his bones and finished what she'd unwittingly started. God, he'd felt good in her hand. Big. Hard. Ready for—

A ring blared from Galen's cell phone on the bedside table, mercifully derailing her thoughts. She felt the heat of his gaze on her as he reached to answer it, and she knew their discussion was far from over.

"Hello." He paused and then covered the receiver with his hand. "It's your lawyer."

She was seriously going to have to think about picking up a new cell. While she didn't relish the idea of talking to her mother anytime soon, it was irresponsible to be out of contact like this, and the guilt was weighing on her. She took the phone. "Hello?"

"Hey, Lacey. I have some news."

"Okay, let me just…" She gave Galen an apologetic smile along with a finger wiggle and climbed out of the bed, making sure to suck in her belly in case he was looking. She crossed the room in search of some privacy. It was impossible to think straight with him staring at her with that *better to eat you with* smile, and something about Allen's tone told her that whatever news he had was worth paying attention to.

She went into the hallway bathroom and closed the door behind her. "Okay, what's up?"

"You're going to love me for this. In fact, you can send the Dom Pérignon to my penthouse."

The Fitzhumes had been friends of the family and she and Allen had had very similar upbringings. They'd both been coerced into attending the same events, taking tennis lessons from the same instructor, and resenting the hell out of it all. She had a reasonable amount of filial affection for him, but in that moment, if he were there she would've popped him in the gut for toying with her. "Stop dancing around and spill it, Fitz!"

"According to the state of Rhode Island, you're not married."

"What do you mean? Reverend Maclan performed the service." Blood rushed to her ears and her legs felt like wet noodles. She sank to the vanity chair and tried not to let hope overtake common sense. "Marty and I both signed the certificate. And I saw the reverend sign it, too."

"Right on both counts. *But…*"

The dramatic pause made Lacey want to jump through the phone and strangle him. She dragged a hand over her face. "You're killing me right now. Killing. Me. Please, just spit it out."

"*Bu-ut*, Reverend Maclan hadn't filed the paperwork yet. There will be a fee involved, which I agreed on your behalf to pay, but I have the unfiled certificate here. We tear it up and *voilà*! It never happened."

She doubled over, suddenly swamped with dizziness. "Are you one hundred percent sure?" she croaked. *Please say yes.* She couldn't take it if this turned out to be some terrible mistake.

"No doubt about it. Once we get off the phone, I'm going to call Marty's lawyer and let him know. You, my dear, are a single woman."

She disconnected and stood. A single woman. Relief sent a cocktail of emotions racing through her, and she started to shake. Hysterical laughter bubbled over and tears sprang to her eyes. Something had finally broken her way, and now there was nothing stopping her from spending the next couple weeks doing the one thing she'd wanted more than anything else. It would hurt when it was over, and she wasn't about to fool herself into thinking it was anything more than a fling, but suddenly it didn't matter.

She made her way to the hall and faced the bedroom door, behind which Whalin' Galen Thomas lay, shirtless and waiting. Like a present, half unwrapped, just for her. She might not be able to satisfy a man like him, but she was going to try her damnedest.

. . .

Galen propped up the pillows and picked up the remote, trying to forget the feel of Lacey's hot little hand wrapped around his cock, pumping away. Jesus, it had been so good, though. Artless but enthusiastic, her grip firm and sure.

He clicked on the TV, desperate for something to distract him from the throbbing in his cock, which showed no signs of abating anytime soon. Commercial in Spanish, commercial in English, The Weather Channel. He stopped there. They'd planned to go hiking in the El Yunque rain forest later that morning, but if the temperature was going to climb above ninety-five, maybe they'd skip it for a day at the casino. Unless she wanted to go back to the beach.

His balls grew tight at the memory of her in her bikini bottoms and he groaned. No, not the beach. Someplace else, where she would be entirely clothed. He was cursing the fact that she hadn't planned to honeymoon in Alaska when the bedroom door swung open again.

"Hey, everything okay?" he asked as Lacey made her way toward the bed. Something about the look on her face made his heart kick, hard. The determined set of her jaw, the gleam in her eye. His instincts were dead-on. One moment she was at the foot of the bed, the next she was airborne. He dropped the remote on the floor just in time to brace himself as she landed on top of him. Air left his lungs in a whoosh, but before he could refill them, she smashed her mouth into his. Their teeth clacked together hard and she drew back, pressing her fingers to her lips.

"Sorry. That was stupid. I could've chipped your tooth or something." Twin red flags bloomed on her cheeks. "Did I chip your tooth?" She pried his mouth open with her thumb and forefinger to inspect his intact enamel.

"My teeth are fine," he said, hoping he sounded less confused than he felt. What could her lawyer have possibly said that would make her jump his bones like that? He was never one to look gift sexual aggression in the mouth, but these ups and downs were wreaking havoc on his libido. "What's going on, Lacey?"

"You don't know?" She flopped off him and onto her back, draping an arm over her face. "God, I can't do anything right. I was trying to seduce you."

He smiled and rolled to face her. "I knew that part, but why? Not that I'm complaining. I want this. Damn, you have no idea how bad I want this, but not if you're going to feel guilty about it in a few hours." He traced her full bottom lip with his thumb, the need to sink his teeth into it almost overwhelming. "Now's the time to decide, though, because I'm about to make it impossible for you to form a coherent thought."

She dropped her arm to her side and turned her head to

face him, the interest in his declaration plain on her face. "I want that. Everybody is always telling me what's best for me, but for the first time, I know what *I* want. And it's you."

It took everything he had not to lift the floodgates and take what she was offering with both hands and, hopefully, his mouth. But he had one more question, more for her peace of mind than his. "What about your husband?"

"I don't have a husband. I have an ex-fiancé. I'm not married," she whispered. "I never was. The certificate hasn't been filed yet, so we can tear it up and it's like it never happened."

Adrenaline coursed through him, and his muscles tingled, every nerve ending snapping to attention. She wet her now trembling lips, her nerves clearly getting the better of her.

He traced the line of her cheekbone with his finger. "That's great. I'm sure you're very relieved." It was a struggle to keep his voice calm, but he needed to pace this right if he wanted it to go down the way he'd imagined. She was ready to dive in, and he was a man on the edge. A couple more clumsy but effective seduction moves out of her and she was going to find herself flat on her back, chock full o' cock, and he would end up reneging on his promise to blow her mind. Then maybe, just maybe, she'd think of him as more than just a fling to help her get over Marty. Maybe they'd have a chance to be something real.

Slow, Galen. Take it nice and slow.

He tipped her chin up and lowered his mouth to hers. A soft, brushing kiss, with only the merest hint of pressure. He pulled back to speak, to tell her all the things he wanted to do to her, but she let out a muffled squeak and used the opportunity to dive in, tangling her tongue with his, nipping, licking, sucking. The force shoved him back against the pillow, and he growled low in his throat. Lacey, wanting and hungry for him, was about the hottest thing he'd ever encountered. The urge to go with it and take her hard and fast clawed at him. His cock jerked as she ground her hips against his in a furious rhythm.

He dragged his mouth away. "You need to give me a minute or this is going to be very disappointing, squirt."

She shook her head, eyes wild. "It couldn't be. I feel like I've been waiting for this forever."

Even more of a reason to make it worth the wait.

If he still had a hope in hell of pulling that off, he was going to have to slow her down a little. Or maybe speed it up and *then* slow it down. His motto was "ladies first" in the bedroom, after all.

In one swift move, he flipped her onto her back. She yelped but adjusted quickly, running her hands over his back and lower, until she had a grip on his ass. He went for her wrists with a pained chuckle, banding them with his fingers. His full weight was distributed between her torso and his knees so his bottom half could get some space, which finally stopped her from grinding her pubic bone against his already rock hard erection.

"Let me go. You're squishing me," she protested, but her pout told a different story.

"I'm not squishing you that much. You just want to maul me some more."

"You don't like it?" Her face fell and he tugged her wrists above her head.

"None of that, squirt. I like it. In fact, I love it. But this" — he angled his hips to her again until his cock nestled against the soft flesh between her thighs; she pulsed against him and he swallowed a curse — "is more than I can bear right now. So we're going to play a little game. It's called No Hands. That means, for the next ten minutes, you can't touch me. At all."

She frowned. "That's a stupid game."

"You only think so because you're a control freak. Humor me, and if you don't like it we never have to play again."

She eyed him for a long moment and then nodded. "Ten minutes." She peered at the clock and then back at him. "Go."

He said a silent prayer of thanks and released her wrists. "Leave them over your head."

She bit her swollen lower lip uncertainly but didn't move. Galen sat back on his heels to look at her. Honey-colored hair decorated the pillow, and he trailed his fingers through its softness.

"I love your hair. It's so fucking sexy. You looked like a mermaid in the water. Want to know a secret?"

Her breath caught and she nodded.

Maybe it would scare her. Maybe she would think he was a total pervert, but she looked so enthralled, so turned on, he couldn't stop the flow of words if he tried. "I've dreamed of you and that hair. Of you taking my cock in your mouth, real slow. Sucking and licking until I felt like I'd explode. And right when I was about to come, I'd wrap my fist in that beautiful hair and use it to work you faster, harder over my cock until I came deep in your throat."

She gasped and her arms came down. "Let me."

Need hit him so hard that his vision blurred and his ears buzzed so loudly he could barely hear. "Ah, babe," he managed to grind out, "you have no idea how much I want to, but I haven't had my ten minutes yet."

Ten had become nine, and he was feeling the pressure. He ran his hand from her wrist, down the length of one arm, over her cheek, to trail down her neck. "Let's get this off," he murmured, tugging the strap of her tank top down to reveal the firm swell of her breast. The sight was too enticing to ignore and he bent low and pressed a kiss there. She smelled like sunshine and flowers and he inhaled deeply. "You smell good enough to eat."

Her whole body was drawn tight, tensed and so ready for what he wanted to give her. He couldn't bring himself to make her wait anymore.

"Fuck it," he said on a groan. He stripped off her dress, yanking it over her head, and moved to her underwear. With a few tugs and a helpful wriggle from Lacey, they were off and on the floor a second later.

There she was. Lacey—naked, ready, and waiting. He'd seen her in sections. Her long, trim legs in the summery dresses she favored. Her pert, softly rounded breasts when she'd lost her bikini in the ocean, then later when he'd caressed them in the pool. The flat expanse of stomach on the beach. But all together, capped off by the neat swatch of honeyed curls between her thighs? It wrecked him. The total silence was marred only by the breath sawing in and out of his lungs.

Ladies first.

He repeated it like a mantra in his head as he grappled for control. Trailing his index finger over one hip and upward, he caressed the lean lines of her body until he reached the very tip of her breast. She hissed, gripping the pillowcase with both hands.

"I can't wait to taste you," he said, leaning into her and flicking out his tongue. He teased her nipple until she strained toward him, back arched in an effort to get more of his mouth. Her response to the slightest touch made him wish he had more mouths, more hands to touch and taste everywhere. He closed his teeth gently over the tight bud and nipped.

"Omigod, yesss."

He cupped her breast and began sucking in earnest, trying to block out her cries as the pressure in his balls built to a heavy ache.

"I can't…you have to…Jesus, Galen, please."

Her nipples were beautifully sensitive and for a fleeting moment, he wondered if he could make her come just from what he was doing. Glancing at the clock, he scratched that idea. He was on borrowed time and she'd never climaxed before. No, they'd do this right.

Pulling back, he gazed down at her flushed face. "I need you to keep your hands up, Lace. No matter what I do, all right? No cheating. I'm on the razor's edge and if you touch me, it's all over."

"Anything. Yes, just…*please*."

Her eyes were glassy with want and they, along with her soft plea, were almost his undoing. He closed his eyes to block out the sight of her and took a steadying breath, then cupped a hand over her pussy and squeezed. The sweet heat drenched his fingers and he groaned as tremors shook him.

Lacey tossed her head restlessly on the pillow and she bounced her hips against his hand. She was more than ready and he slid one finger down her center, working the slick, tender flesh until her muttered cries became a litany.

"Galen, yeah, oh God, yeah."

"I need to put my mouth on you. I'm starving for the taste of that wet little pussy." His words were barely coherent, his voice was so rough. Continuing to stroke her, he slid down the bed until his face was level with her hips, then he dipped his head low. His heart pounded like a jackhammer as he ran his tongue along her seam. When the taste of her flooded his mouth, he lost his mind, sucking and licking, rubbing her swollen clit with his tongue as he thrust one finger into her gripping core.

The jolt of desire was almost electric. So fucking tight. So fucking wet. Then her hands were in his hair, holding him fast, sealing his mouth to her. Her thighs gripped his head, muffling her screams as the orgasm hit her. Her body tensed, legs trembling as she came against his lips, her clutching heat squeezing his finger like a fist as he slid it in and out. Need battered at him like a tidal wave, the urge to feel that tight channel closing over his cock over and over until he exploded inside her, sucking him under.

"That's, oh, wow. I didn't think I could, but… Now I get it. I so get it," she said, gasping for air. Her fingers still had his hair in a death grip and her legs twitched. In spite of the need grinding at him, he wanted to stand up and do a victory lap.

"You ain't seen nothin' yet, squirt."

"I don't know if I can handle better than that." She quivered as he gently pulled away. "Please, stay with me. I want—"

"Condom and I'll be right back," he said, then rolled to his feet.

"No," she gasped, sitting up to take his arm. "I'm on the Pill if you…" She trailed off, her bourbon eyes still hot with need.

Her trust in him was humbling and he owed her no less. It was liberating to be with someone who he had a history with and could depend on not to try to trap him or trick him. *Only with Lacey.* "I'm safe. This is a first for me," he admitted and moved to crawl back into the bed with her.

"Wait. The thing you said before. About my hair? I… really want to do that." She wet her lips and shimmied down the bed until her mouth was a scant inch from his tackle. His body went into lockdown mode, as if central command had pulled the plug. His mind bellowed, *Back away*, but his cock was clearly the stronger force, because nothing short of a grenade could've gotten him to budge. Almost in slow motion, her pink tongue peeked out for a swipe over the head of his cock.

"Mmm," she murmured, taking him in her hand and dropping to her haunches as if settling in.

"Lacey," he protested weakly, reaching out a hand to pull her away. But she took his hand and buried it into her hair, wrapping her fist around his until he held her in a punishing grip. His balls drew tight against his body. "You don't have to do this."

She peered up at him and smiled. "I know. But I want to." Then she sucked him in hard, cheeks hollowing as she drew deep, deeper until he hit the soft flesh at the back of her throat. She let go of his hand, but her assistance was no longer needed as he worked her over his cock by that sexy mane of hair. The tight, wet suction was a siren's song too seductive to escape. All too soon, he felt it. The cum pooling low in his balls, the tension low and tight in his belly.

"We've got to stop or I'm going to come." His warning fell on deaf ears, because he tugged at her hair, but she just kept on going. In fact, she was moving more quickly, her head bobbing between his legs. "Fuck," he growled, and then he exploded into the molten cavern of her mouth, holding her to him as he spurted hard into her throat.

Chapter Eight

Dreaming. Surely she was dreaming. Galen stood in front of her, all big, hard muscles, his face a mask of pleasure so keen it could've been pain. She lapped the soft, broad head one last time.

"So good," he muttered as he released his grip on her hair and trailed a gentle finger over her cheek.

"I had no idea," she said, wondering if he could even hear her over the pounding of her heart.

He pulled her to her feet and wrapped his arms tightly around her waist, holding her close. "That's the tip of the iceberg. There's so much more."

She nuzzled his throat, breathing in the musky scent of him with a happy sigh. "I want to. I want it all." Emboldened by his attention, she wriggled in his arms, letting her nipples drag through the light smattering of hair on his chest.

"Nice," he hissed, and slid his hands lower to cup her bottom. He tilted his hips into her, his already thickening member prodding her belly. A tendril of fresh need curled in her belly. And then her stomach growled.

"How about breakfast?" he asked with a chuckle, giving

her bottom a playful slap.

Who knew good sex was such hungry business? She stepped back and glanced down at his increasing erection. "Are you sure you don't want to?" She waggled her eyebrows and took him in hand for a gentle squeeze.

"We have all day, and if what we just did was any indication, we're both going to need the fuel."

His dark eyes held a sensual promise that almost made her forget the food altogether. Then her stomach growled again and he chuckled. "I make a mean ham on rye," he said, tossing her his T-shirt.

"For breakfast?"

"I have three things in my repertoire. Sandwiches, steak on the grill, and protein shakes. Take your pick."

"Ham on rye it is."

He slipped on his boxers and they made their way into the kitchen, laughing like teenagers.

While he fixed the sandwiches, she cut up a mango and poured some juice to go with it.

"Tell me what it was like with Marty."

She curled her lip and winced. "Ugh, seriously? Why would you want to hear that?"

"I can't get my head around a guy being with a woman who looks like this"—he waved a hand up and down in her direction—"who is so sexual and responsive, and leaving it on the table that way. It's a sacrilege," he said with an incredulous shake of his head.

She set the knife down and tugged at the hem of her shirt self-consciously. "I think you're biased because of our… recent activities. I don't think anyone has ever referred to me as sexy."

"You are, though." He took the cap off the mustard and smeared some on their bread.

"It's not blatant or even intentional, but it's there. The way you move and in your expressive, curious face. All that was missing was a guy smart enough to see it and want to coax it out to play."

To play. She couldn't forget that part. This was all for fun.

He sliced the sandwiches in half and set their plates on the granite island before sitting on one of the stools. "Let's eat."

She moved to sit on the opposite stool, but he pulled her to the space between his legs so she was leaning against him. "I feel like I need to be close to you right now. Humor me."

A warm thrill ran through her at his words, but she tamped it down to a trickle. She wouldn't take every little thing he said and read something into it. She would seize the frigging day and enjoy her time here. Then, and not until then, she would think about what the future held for her.

They ate their sandwiches in companionable silence. When they finished, he plucked up a piece of mango and held it to her mouth.

She took it from between his fingers with her teeth, lapping a drop of juice from his thumb with her tongue.

"That will be burned in my memory forever," he said in a low, husky voice that made her nipples go hard.

"Wh-what will?"

"Of you. Giving me head so enthusiastically. So fucking good."

She subconsciously shifted to thrust her bottom against him, enflamed by his words. He groaned his approval and took her hips in a tight grip. "Turn around." It sounded like a challenge, and it was one she was more than happy to accept.

She turned in his arms, and he slipped his hand around her neck, pressing two fingers to her pulse. "I see how you want me, and I can't even describe how hard it gets me."

The intensity of his gaze threatened to swallow her whole. She looked away. "You make me feel beautiful."

"You *are* beautiful."

Her heart swelled in her chest, and she pressed her forehead to his for fear of him seeing the truth in her eyes. She was in love with him already, if she hadn't been before, and it terrified her. He snaked his hand around to her nape and captured her lips with his. The kiss was tender, sweet, almost reverent. And then it wasn't. Like a wildfire blazing from the smallest of embers, it raged out of control. He nipped at her lower lip until she opened for him, then soothed the tender spot with his tongue. His free hand crept around her waist and shoved the cotton shirt up so he could touch her skin.

He released her mouth and stood, kicking the stool out from behind him. It hit the counter with a crash.

The T-shirt was up and over her head in a flash, and in one move he'd lifted her onto the island. She gasped as the cool granite hit her skin, scalding with need.

"Galen?"

His eyes had gone almost black, and his gaze raked her from head to toe. He was like a man possessed. Dropping to a crouch, he draped her thighs over his broad shoulders and pressed a palm to her belly, easing her back until she was open to him, supporting herself on her hands.

"I can see how wet you are, slick and ready for me."

His warm breath washed over her clit, his whispered words shaking her to the core, and she whimpered.

"Yes. So ready."

Just the anticipation of him sliding deep inside her made her heart flutter. How could she be so turned on when he'd barely touched her this time?

Her thought blew away like feathers on the beach as he pressed two fingers to her and thrust deep. Sensation overwhelmed her, and she cried out, scrabbling at the countertop with her nails. A moment later, he bent and covered her with his tongue, lapping then sucking. She couldn't help but chant his name and arch against his mouth. More. She would die if he didn't give her more. And like magic, he did, quickening the pace, licking and suckling harder and faster.

Her body tensed, poised for climax, and she froze. "Please, Galen. With you this time. Please."

He tore his mouth away and slid his fingers from her. "Fuck yeah."

Supporting her legs, he slid them off his shoulders and stood. He peered down between them, a feral smile spread across his lips. "You're so sweet, I could stay down there forever," he said, spreading her thighs wide. "But I need to be inside you so bad."

He didn't bother taking off his boxers. Instead, he shoved them over his hips until his cock thrust forward, bumping against her thigh. She watched, breathless, as he closed his hand over himself and he looked up, noting her rapt attention.

"You like what you see?" he asked, gripping himself tighter and stroking his shaft from base to tip.

She couldn't keep the strangled groan from escaping her lips and her eyes shot to his. "Is that weird?"

"Weird that you like to watch me touch myself?" he asked, frowning. "Are you kidding me? You're my wet dream come to life."

He did it again, working himself in one long jerk, then squeezing. Her breath came in pants as he moved faster and faster and his erection swelled to the point that she knew a moment of fear.

"The look on your face right now is almost worth making myself come all over your thighs and stomach, but I have to be inside you." His voice sounded like he'd taken a karate chop to the throat. "I'll go slow."

She looked up. "I-I think I'd like that sometime. For you to...do that on my stomach," she said before she could change her mind about saying it.

He groaned and stepped closer, lining the swollen head of his cock up with her entrance. He pressed forward, inch by excruciating inch. Full, she felt so full, but he continued until her body resisted, the depths unyielding.

"You are so goddamned tight, babe. I can't—" When he paused, her body relaxed and stretched around him. He pulsed and twitched deep inside her, and she moaned. He spoke through gritted teeth. "You good? Am I hurting you?"

She shook her head, too taken by the sensation of having him inside her to speak. Jerking her hips toward him, she urged him forward. With a growl he withdrew, then drove in hard and deep. She came instantly, her orgasm crashing over her as she cried out his name. The aftershock still rocked her when he began to move. Slow at first, a shallow thrust, then deeper until his pubic bone ground against her clit with every plunge. She opened her eyes and looked down to the place where their bodies were joined. Where his heavy sex, glossy with her juices, moved in and out of her, faster and faster. He gripped her thigh, his movements becoming frantic, and he grew impossibly harder inside her.

"With me, Lacey," he groaned and pressed a finger to her clit.

The touch went through her like lightning. She sobbed and broke apart, the column of her sex clamping over him. He tumbled after her, gritting his teeth then bellowing her name as he jerked deep inside her. When their quivers subsided, he pulled her into his arms and she wrapped her legs around his waist, holding him tight, pressing soft kisses against his shoulder.

With me, Lacey, he'd said.

If only he'd meant forever.

Chapter Nine

It was evening by the time they emerged from the bedroom again. He tugged Lacey into the shower, and she laughed, hiding her face in his shoulder, trying to shield herself from him.

"I just spent the better part of the day kissing, licking, and sucking every part of you, and you're going to get shy again? No way." He kissed her hard and pulled away until he could see her entire body. She blushed, but she didn't turn away.

Funny how he'd been on a mission to drive her wild. He'd succeeded, and had the scratches on his back to prove it. But what he hadn't expected was for her to drive him just as crazy. Hell, she'd knocked him flat on his ass. Giving and greedy. Sensual but sweet. He'd never been with anyone like her.

"What are you thinking about?" she asked, swiping the wet hair from her face.

"Taking you out," he said. It was the truth. He wanted to take her on the town in a pretty dress and open doors for her. She deserved to be doted on some.

"Where?"

"I don't know. Let's get ready for a special night, and we'll go down and talk to the concierge. Maybe dinner and the casino?"

She shook her head and held up a hand. "I'm not really a gambler, but I'll watch if you want to go."

"We'll figure something out. Now go get ready." He gave her one more quick kiss and shooed her out of the stall.

After he dried off and dressed, he waited in the living room while she did whatever face-painting, boob-taping ritual girls did to get ready for a fancy night out. An hour later he was just about to start complaining when she walked into the living room and sent his jaw swinging.

Her honey-colored mane swung loose around her bare shoulders, framing her glowing face beautifully. The black dress she'd chosen was shorter than anything he'd ever seen her wear and showed off her gorgeous gams to perfection. "Damn, squirt. You are so fine."

Her hand fluttered to her midriff and she looked away. "Yeah, well, thank your sister. She insisted that every girl needs a little black dress—emphasis on the 'little'—and she made me buy it for the honeymoon."

"Remind me to send her some flowers."

He hustled her out the door before she changed her mind and her clothes, and they made their way to the main hall reception desk.

"Good evening, Jesus. We were hoping you could offer some suggestions for a big night on the town."

"Oh, hello Mr. and Mrs. Clemson. I was going to come to you today, but things got very busy here at the desk. You had some more phone calls." He ruffled through some papers on his desk and held out a pile of messages.

She eyed them like they'd been dipped in acid. "All of them from my mother?"

He shrugged then nodded. "Yes. She, ah, really wants you

to call her, I think."

Lacey straightened her shoulders and smiled at him. "You can just chuck those in the trash. In fact, unless something important comes through, you don't have to bring them up to me anymore. No need for a special trip. I think I got the gist yesterday."

Galen took her hand and gave it an approving squeeze.

"If you insist, ma'am." Jesus looked almost comically relieved and he tossed the pile in the garbage can behind the desk. "Now, for this evening, would you like to salsa, maybe?"

"God, no!" Lacey said with a violent shake of her head. "Too hard. Maybe just a little place where we can sway together and have a cocktail."

"Let me give you a list of places." He pulled out a sheet of paper and slid it over the counter. "Another thought is the dinner cruise. They have two each evening, and the second one is scheduled to leave in thirty minutes. People say good things about it, and it offers a little of everything. Gambling, entertainment, dinner, and a great view."

Galen sent Lacey a questioning glance.

She nodded. "Sounds like fun, and it's a beautiful night."

Armed with directions, they made the fifteen-minute walk to the ship. It was small, large enough for maybe fifty people, but it was luxuriously appointed with teak railings that gleamed in the fading evening sunlight.

The host welcomed them onboard, then sat them for dinner with a wide smile. "Your waiter will be here with our cocktail specials and wine list in just a moment. Enjoy!"

They thanked him and settled into their cozy booth, taking in the view of the island from the water. The room was open on all sides, and a balmy breeze kicked up as the ship pulled away from the pier.

An hour, two beers, and a plate of *guanimes* later, Lacey

paused with a spoonful of flan halfway to her lips, her brows raised in outrage.

"So that's why Jimmy MacTurk called me Lacey Drawers."

Her retelling of the childhood memory had him grinning. "That's a pretty good reason for the nickname. I mean, if you're going to go around flashing your bloomers at him." He shrugged.

"I wasn't flashing him! I was just riding on the seesaw. He was a little perv, is all."

He laughed, and she joined him, dropping the mock annoyance. "I have so much fun with you," she said softly.

He nodded and took her hand. "Right back at you."

They stared stupidly at each other, grinning like fools, until their waiter came to take their plates.

"Good choice," she said on a sigh. "This ship is really lovely."

He stood and took her hand. "Shall we see what else it has to offer?"

"Definitely."

Full from their meal, they took their time strolling the perimeter of the boat, stopping to greet other couples and take in the view. They passed a wide set of doors and a slow, sensual beat caught his ear. He tugged her toward it. "Maybe they have a band playing and we can do some dancing. Come on."

She resisted, digging in her heels. "I don't think that's a good idea. I'm a terrible dancer."

"Well, I'm not, and I can teach you."

"Seriously?"

"Yeah. My first trainer thought partnered dancing was a great tool to prep fighters. Learning how to lead, anticipating the move of your partner and all that, but it's also great for stamina and balance. So I took some classes, and it stuck with me. At first I thought it was bullshit, but I think it's actually helped me over the years."

"Great, so you'll look cool as usual. I'm going to look like an idiot, though. Your sister and I bop around and stuff at the clubs once in a while, but if you're talking like the stuff they do in *Dirty Dancing*? I'm pretty sure my hips don't move like that." Her brow wrinkled the way it did when she got anxious, and he pressed a kiss to that spot.

"After the last ten hours, I can vouch for the fact that they definitely do."

She rolled her eyes. "Not the same thing. But," she said, sucking in a deep breath, "I'll try it. As long as you promise if I hate it we can leave and try to find shuffleboard or something."

"Deal."

When he opened the door to the club, the song changed and Lacey visibly paled. "What is that, swing?" She froze. "I-I don't know, Galen. Why don't we just go sit on deck and enjoy the breeze?"

"No way. I want to spin you around and show you off. It's going to be great," he assured her and wrapped an arm around her shoulders. "We can watch for a while and you tell me when you're ready. We can start with a slow song. Swaying, like you said."

"Okay." She allowed him to lead her through the wide entryway and down the red-carpeted steps into the large room. The lights were low and inviting, flickering off the teakwood bar and tables. A large dance floor loomed in the center of the room. Lacey stiffened beside him. It wasn't very crowded. Maybe twenty milled around the edge, all seeming to wait for that one couple to take the leap first. Most were dressed similar to Lacey, with cocktail dresses or skirts, and men in sports jackets and jeans.

"Let's sit and have a drink," he said, pulling her over to a small table by the dance floor. Before the waitress had come to take their orders, the song that was playing ended, and the DJ called into the microphone.

"I want to thank everyone for coming out tonight to our ballroom dance night. Let's keep things rolling with a cha-cha. Any beginners here? We have two dancers on staff who would be happy to teach anyone who'd like to learn."

The small crowd chattered, but no one stepped up.

"You want a lesson from the pro?" he asked.

Lacey shook her head furiously. "No way. You said you would teach me."

The DJ continued. "How about any intermediate dancers? Looking for a partner and want to dance with either Yesenia or Junior?" He gestured to an attractive pair seated next to the DJ booth who smiled and waved.

Lacey grabbed his arm and shook it hard. "Get up there. Go dance so I can at least see what I'm getting into."

"I came to dance with you."

"And you will, but I need a minute to settle down. Plus I'm a visual learner, and it will be easier for me to pick it up if I see it." Her wide eyes pleaded with him.

"I know you're only doing this to buy yourself some time, but don't think you're getting off the hook. You swear if I go up, you'll dance with me next?"

She bit her lip then nodded. "Swear."

An older woman had already scooped up Junior, and Yesenia turned to speak to the DJ when Galen called out. "I'll give it a whirl."

The dancer smiled and stood, gliding toward him, hips swaying like a Latin ballroom dancer's should.

"Well, crap," Lacey muttered.

"What's the matter now?" he asked with a short laugh. "You're the one who wanted me to do it."

"Yeah, well, she didn't look all that impressive sitting over there, but I didn't realize she was going to be sex on a stick walking over here."

"You want me to say no?"

Yesenia beckoned from the edge of the dance floor and Lacey blew out a sigh. "No, go ahead. Better her than me right now."

The strains of "Will You Still Love Me Tomorrow" blared from the house speakers and, in spite of his bravado, he felt like a kid on his first day of school. Nervous, and hoping he had the goods to impress. "Here goes nothing."

. . .

Galen had lied. He knew far more than the basics. They started with the standard old "One, two, cha-cha-cha," but fairly quickly, Yesenia caught on to the fact that Galen was no beginner. And now? He and the sensual brunette were tearing up the floor. The crowd gathered around and even Junior and his partner stopped to watch. Galen was masterful, and his partner's cheeks flushed with pleasure when he spun her around twice. Son of a gun, he was good. He executed a stunning lift and Yesenia laughed out loud. His body was so fit, he made it look easy, and jealousy reared its ugly head.

Lacey was sure she wouldn't enjoy a second of this. It looked too impulsive, too unrestrained, too dangerous. Then, about halfway through, the dance sucked her in. The fact that Galen's eyes met hers a dozen times, with a hint of challenge and a lot of promise, definitely helped. He was dancing with Yesenia, she of the well-oiled caboose, but he was dancing *for* Lacey.

The song ended, and the pair bowed to the audience's applause. Yesenia thanked Galen and brought him back to the table.

"You are a very lucky woman," she said with a smile, before sauntering off to find another partner.

"That was…amazing," she admitted ruefully. "It's ludicrous that a man your size, who beats up other men your size for a living, could move like that."

"You like?" Galen held out a hand and grinned. "Well get in on this, then."

She stared up into his smiling brown eyes, wanting so badly not to disappoint him, but she was almost paralyzed with fear. Her hands had gone icy cold and she couldn't feel her lips. What if she made a total fool of herself? What if she fell on these cursed heels and broke her coccyx bone? A dozen excuses marched to the tip of her tongue, ready for deployment, when he cupped her chin in his big, warm hand.

"Hey. Stop this. I got you, okay?"

He caressed her cheek with his thumb and the fear began to melt. She wanted this. She wanted to be in Galen's arms, hips swaying to the beat. She wanted him to twirl her and dip her and to shimmy her shoulders until his eyes popped out. And she was done not taking what she wanted.

She grabbed his hand and pulled him onto the far corner of the dance floor. "Teach me."

"Rockin' Robin" came on, and she stared up at Galen expectantly.

"Let's jive, baby."

They started off slow, and at first, she was aware of everyone around her. Were they looking? Laughing? But no sooner had she realized that no one was paying attention to her at all, that it no longer mattered. All that mattered was Galen, and the way he made her feel. When she stumbled, he caught her, holding on a little longer and a little tighter than he needed to. When she made a mistake, he showed her again, endlessly patient until she felt comfortable. By the end of the night, she'd gotten the hang of the basics of several dances and was ready to try for real, in the center of the floor. It felt like kismet when the last song was one she knew well.

"'The Stroll.' I love this song!" she said with a grin.

"Then we'd better get out there." He led her to the middle of the floor and stepped back, leaving her in a line with six other women and taking his place next to their male counterparts. Although they were apart, stepping and sliding in their respective rows, his eyes never left hers. The heat of his gaze made her feel beautiful, so she tossed her hair back and put a little extra sway in her hips. By the time it was their turn to meet in the middle, she was desperate for his touch. He cupped her waist, and their hips rocked together, perfectly synchronized, as they strolled down the center of the floor.

Every so often, accidentally on purpose, she brushed her breast to his chest or her thigh against his, and the hand on her waist would tighten, his eyes going dark. The power was heady, and she wielded it with glee.

When the song ended, they stopped to applaud the other dancers, breathless and smiling. It hadn't been flawless, but it was perfect and she felt like she was dancing on air. If this time was all they could ever have, she would always be grateful to at least have these memories. She rose on her tiptoes and kissed him hard on the mouth. "Thank you," she whispered.

• • •

The next five days with Galen were heaven. The next five nights? Heaven during Mardi Gras. Overtly sensual, steamy, and totally erotic. No matter how many times they did it, their lovemaking was mind-blowing. Galen seemed driven to take her to new heights and his hunger was insatiable.

They'd fallen into a routine of waking early and going to the main resort for a workout. He taught her how to jump rope, and she taught him Pilates, although the latter had prompted them to cut their workout short when he requested a private lesson in the nude.

Her favorite thing, though, was watching him shadowbox. After his weight training, he always went into a corner and started swinging. She would be on the elliptical machine, peering from beneath her lashes while he dipped and turned, bobbed and weaved, rocking forward on the balls of his feet. He wasn't a brawler like so many thick fighters were, rolling their shoulders and crabbing flat-footed around the ring, on the hunt for a chance to land that one stunning blow. He was a boxer, quick, sharp, always moving, sticking, and jabbing. The commentators liked to say that, by the time Whalin' Galen knocked out his opponents, they were likely glad for the respite. He was beautiful to watch and moved with such fluidity, such grace, it wasn't until he stood next to a mortal man that his size became apparent.

During the third workout, she finally got the nerve to ask him. "Will you show me?"

He swiped a muscled forearm over his sweaty brow and gave her a lethal grin. "Darlin', I'm not sure what you're referring to, but I can't imagine saying no to anything you want to see."

His words sent a thrill through her, and she tamped back the urge to blurt, *Seriously? Why me?* The words seemed to be ever-present on the tip of her tongue. Still, she managed to keep it in because the answer wouldn't change anything. He could've had a fling with anyone on the island, but he'd picked her. In this magical place, at this magical moment, she had found happiness, and she was going to hold on with both fists until it was over.

"I want to learn how to box."

When his smile broadened, she congratulated herself for finally speaking up.

"For real?"

"Yeah. I've been watching forever but never thought about it as a workout. I'd really like to learn."

He cocked his head to the side. "After all the years we've known each other, I can't get over how you continue to surprise me." His dark eyes held hers captive. "I've never had a woman interested in my career before, aside from the celebrity of it. I gotta tell you, it's very sexy."

Warmth spread through her whole body, as if she'd turned to face the sun. "Teach me. I want to know everything."

He chuckled, and she rushed to correct herself. "I mean, I know we don't have a lot of time, but whatever you can show me in a week." The last thing she wanted was for him to think he was going to have to let her down easy once they went back home. She might be naive in some aspects, but she wasn't a total rube. When they went back to Rhode Island, they would be leaving this behind. The thought was like an eclipse, sapping the warmth of the sun away. She shoved it aside in a rush.

Galen rubbed his hands together and grinned. "I am so down with this plan; I can't wait to start. We'll see if we can't find a sporting goods store to get me some punch mitts and you some wraps and little gloves. It's going to be a blast."

She drew back. "I just meant fooling around here. I didn't know we needed stuff for it. You don't need to go through all that trouble for me."

He shook his head with a frown. "When are you going to get it, Lacey? You're worth the trouble. You deserve to be around people who want to do things for you and make you smile." His face softened and he pulled her in for a hug.

"Besides, this isn't for you, it's for both of us. I'm really looking forward to it."

She held him tightly, reveling in the clean sweat smell of him, until he reached down and smacked her on the ass.

"In fact, let's start now. I'll teach you some moves. Come on." He stepped back an arm's length. "First thing, let's get your stance right. You're a southpaw, right?"

"Well, I've never punched anyone before, but I write with my left hand, yes."

"Okay, so usually you stand in front of a mirror for this part, but since you're a southpaw and I'm not, I can be your mirror." He waggled his brows at her and she smiled. "Start in athletic position, feet shoulder-width apart, knees slightly bent."

She did as he said and then looked up at him. "Like this?"

"Close, but not flat like that. Get up on the balls of your feet, get a little movement going."

She tried to mimic him, bouncing on her toes, but she felt like a total idiot and stopped. "I don't think I—"

"That was great, come on. Keep doing it."

She did, reluctantly at first, but more enthusiastically at his approving grin.

"Nice. Watch me, and do what I do."

He moved his right foot back a step, swiveling his hips at a forty-five-degree angle and she followed suit.

"Nope," he said, reaching out to pat her thigh. "I'm your mirror. I put my right foot back and lead with my left. You do the opposite. Like a mirror, got it?"

She switched feet and waited for his next command.

"And don't stop bouncing, gotta keep it moving. Good. You're still too straight on, though. Tilt your hips more, get almost sideways. Stand like you were, and you're a wall, just waiting to get hit. Get on the angle and you're a much smaller target." He twisted to show her, exaggerating the move, and flashing his tight butt for the second before he turned back to her.

She twisted until her stance matched his. "Good?"

"Beautiful." He lifted his left hand up and made a loose fist. "Lift your right up. Not so high. You're blocking your line of sight. Put it right below eye level. That way you're covering most of your face, but you can see what you're aiming at and what's coming."

She dropped her hand down a little.

"Good. That's your jabbing hand. A jab is the feeler punch. A tester. The soldier you send out to get the lay of the land. Tire the other guy out some, keep them guessing. Now put up the left. This one's going to be level with your chin, elbow more bent and closer to your body."

She followed his lead and sent him a questioning glance.

"Right. This is your power punching hand. The mac daddy. The haymaker. It's cocked and ready to fire, like a piston. The strength of your whole body will be behind it, but because you expend so much energy to throw, you have to limit it. Make every single one count. You ready to throw some punches?"

His biceps bunched and gleamed with sweat and she tore her gaze away to meet his. What she saw there nearly took her breath away. The boyish smile, his face lit up in the best way…a swell of emotion rolled through her, so strong she wanted to throw herself in his arms and beg him to never let her go. Instead she nodded. "Let's do it."

"The most important weapon in boxing is the jab. There isn't a truly great fighter out there, alive or dead, who didn't have an effective jab. You want to skip a step forward with your right foot, getting a little of your body behind it when you let that fist snap out, okay? When the fist comes back, so should the foot."

His hand flicked out, so fast it was a blur. She dropped her hands and jumped back.

"Never put your hands down. Come on, I wasn't even close to you. Get back in here. You try."

She tried to put it all together, bounce, fist at eye level, step forward, let her hand fly—

"Not bad! But don't let it linger like that. You leave it out there, you're wide open to a right cross. You'd get your block knocked off. Fast, like a viper." He took her wrist and guided her, snapping her fist against his palm hard and quickly pulling it back.

She repeated the motion alone, and this time he barked out a laugh. "Woo-hoo, baby girl! That's what I'm talking about. You're like lightning. But we gotta get a little something behind it."

"You said this was the feeler punch. I thought—"

"Right. But every punch should come with bad intentions and the jab is no different. Whether it's to disarm or disorient, you've got to make sure there's enough juice behind it to make your opponents take notice. If not, they won't need to expend any energy worrying about it, and your odds of getting off a real clock-cleaner when they aren't looking shrink exponentially."

And so it went. He was a patient and thorough teacher, which was no surprise given his demeanor in the bedroom, but he was also demanding. It had brought out the best in her. He'd complimented her on her speed and agility more than once, swearing that she was a natural. Her nerves and the initial fear of looking foolish disappeared and her confidence soared. She'd had the time of her life, and an hour later they'd fallen into a happy, exhausted heap on the floor, promising to do it again the next day.

They went upstairs to shower, and she'd just taken hers

when there was a knock at the door. "Did you order room service?" she called into the bathroom to Galen. He must not have heard her over the spray because he didn't respond. She shrugged and crossed the room to open the front door.

Cat stood there, decked out in a sundress and floppy hat. Her green eyes sparkled, and she tossed her hat in the air with a shout. "Woo-hoo! Good morning, Puerto Rico-oh-oh!" She dropped her suitcase to drag Lacey in for a bear hug.

"Holy crap," she said, limp with shock as her friend attempted to squeeze her guts out. "What are you doing here?"

"I figured you had a whole week left, and my brother was probably driving you crazy by now. I finished up my project at the office and thought I'd come save you and work on my tan. Awesome, no?" She pulled back, beaming with excitement.

She was right about one thing. Galen was driving her crazy. All night, every night. As glad as she was to see her friend, a big part of her was heartsick over the loss of alone time with Galen. She'd been banking on that week, counting and recounting the hours like a miser with his chest of gold, and now it was gone, just like that. Surely Galen wouldn't want his sister to know what they'd been up to. That would make it too real, and this was nothing more than a fantasy.

Her throat felt thick, and she fought to find a smile for her best friend in the world. "Awesome is right. I'm so happy you're here." She grabbed Cat's suitcase and pulled her into the villa. "How was your flight?"

"Long but super smooth, thanks. I'm starving, though. What's with this five hours in the air and no in-flight meal crap? Is that a new thing?" She dropped onto the couch with a grateful sigh. "I was ready to give myself to the pilot for another sad little bag of nuts."

"Who are you kidding? You're a sucker for a man in

uniform. I think the peanuts would've been optional."

Cat snort-laughed and nodded. "You're probably right. I didn't get a look at him, though, so I can't say for sure." She held out a handful of papers. "These are for you. The chubby little guy at the front desk asked me to bring them."

Lacey rolled her eyes. "Awesome."

"What are they?"

"Notes from my mother. Whoever is at the front desk probably didn't get the memo that I don't want them. Other than these? It's been great. We don't have phone or Internet here, and she hasn't been able to get her paws on Galen's cell number, so she's taken to calling the front desk with scathing messages for me." She tossed them, unread, onto the coffee table.

Galen sauntered into the room in a pair of threadbare gym shorts, scrubbing his damp hair with a towel. "Hey, did you see where my camera w—" His eyes bugged out a little when his sister stood. "Holy shit, what are you doing here, runt?" Although he sounded happy to see her, there was a split second where his face dropped.

Lacey's heart felt a little lighter for it. Maybe he wasn't quite ready to let go, either.

"Came to check on my girl and make sure you weren't boring her to tears with sports talk or driving her to drink with your terrible jokes."

He slung the towel over his shoulder, leaving his bare chest and eight-pack abs in plain view. "Let's ask her. Am I boring you to tears yet, squirt?" There was no mistaking the challenge in his voice. As if he were daring her to tell Cat exactly what had been going on between them.

She swallowed hard and shook her head. "N-not really. We've been…sparring."

He grinned and nodded slowly, still not breaking eye

contact with her. "We *have* been doing that."

Cat whipped her head toward Lacey, then to Galen, and back again before she held up a hand. She made a noise that sounded either like a muffled scream or like the squeal of tires coming to a halt. "Hold up." She wrinkled her nose as if she'd just been handed week-old fish stuffed inside the dirty tube sock of a teenage boy. "You two are… Are you? Oh, ew. Just…just fucking ew." She speared her hands into her copper-colored hair and blew out a sigh. "When?"

"What do you mean, when?" Galen asked, chuckling. "Last night. The night before. The night before that. This morning." He'd ticked off each instance on his fingers and sent Lacey a broad wink at the last one. She groaned and buried her face in her hands.

"I meant," Cat said, enunciating crisply while treating her brother to a death stare, "when did it start, moron."

Galen shrugged, the picture of nonchalance as he made his way into the kitchen. "Last week. When we found out Lacey wasn't really married." He ignored her outraged gasp and started taking out fixings for a ham sandwich.

Cat wheeled on Lacey. "A week? You've been boning my brother for a week and you didn't think to mention it? Sisters before misters, remember, Lace? We're supposed to tell each other everything."

The hurt in her voice made Lacey feel like gum on the bottom of a shoe and she scrambled to explain. "We didn't come here with this in mind. It just sort of…happened."

"Oh, geez, now you sound like Marty. You don't bang someone by accident." Lacey opened her mouth to clarify, but Cat cut her off. "Nope. I don't need to hear any more. It doesn't matter. You're both adults, and you have the right to do what you want with whom you want, no matter how much it grosses me out. I wish you had told me when it first happened, though."

Lacey nodded miserably. What was there to say? Cat was right. They'd never had secrets between them before. How could she explain that what she was experiencing with Galen felt so tenuous, so fragile that she was afraid even the slightest disturbance would make it disappear? That the time they had was so short and precious, she didn't want to waste a second of it on the telephone justifying it. But she couldn't say either of those things because Galen was in the room with them, and he didn't deserve that kind of pressure from her.

"We should have said something. And if we planned to continue with this in our real lives, we likely would have, but this stays in Puerto Rico. Once we're home, everything goes back to normal," Lacey said, trying with all her might to sound brisk and matter-of-fact. A statement, not a question, because that would be pitiful. She could almost feel the weight of Galen's heavy gaze on her. *Back to normal*. Why did that sound so God awful now? Maybe because normal meant no making love on the kitchen counter. No snuggling up on the beach to watch the sunset. No boxing until the sweat stung her eyes and her heart felt like it was going to pound out of her chest.

Normal meant no Galen.

"So this is purely sexual?" Cat asked, the curl of her lip revealing her feelings on the subject.

Galen fielded that one. "You know what it is? None of your business. Now quit grilling Lacey and get unpacked. I'll make you a sandwich, and then we can figure out our plans for the rest of the day."

Cat allowed Lacey to lead her into the guest room. When Lacey closed the door behind them, Cat turned to face her. "You don't blame me for being shocked, do you? I mean, I always knew there was some weird attraction between you two, but I never saw this coming." She sank back on the bed with a dazed shake of her head.

"Weird attraction? On my end, maybe, but he went out of his way to torture me."

"As teenage boys do when they like someone."

"I don't think so, Cat."

"That's okay. We do better when you let me do the thinking for you, and I'm telling you that he didn't treat my other friends that way."

"Oh yeah? How did he treat them?" She busied herself straightening the pillows on the bed, as if the answer didn't matter in the least, but her hands were shaking. If Galen liked her before, maybe there was a chance…

"Like they were invisible, mostly. Like Becca."

Lacey couldn't help the flinch.

"I know. She's a buddy-fucker and I'm thinking of making a voodoo doll of her. Sorry I mentioned her name. But he never gave her the time of day. He wasn't that way with you. He teased you a lot, but it was never mean-spirited, you know? There always seemed to be affection behind it." She tugged at Lacey's arm to stop her fussing. "If it matters any, you have my blessing. I'm still trying to get my head around it all, but I love you guys to heaven and back, and as long as you both feel the same way about each other, I think it would be really cool. You guys being a couple."

She realized then that, even without Galen in the room, telling Cat about her growing feelings toward him was not an option. Already Cat was investing too much into it, and if things didn't work out, and she knew how Lacey felt, she'd be mad at him. That wasn't fair to Galen at all. He'd never made any promises or given her false hope for a future together. It was better for Cat to think she felt the same way he did. "I appreciate that, truly, but we're not… It's not like that. We haven't talked about anything beyond the next week. He was here when I needed someone, and he opened my eyes about a lot of things. But his goal was to help me through a tough time, and he did that. I already owe him more than you could ever imagine."

Cat's eyes narrowed. "Really? You're trying to tell me you slept with someone you have no feelings for?"

Lacey couldn't bring herself to lie outright, so she worded her answer carefully. "I'm trying to tell you that this was an impulse. The result of two people in an emotionally charged situation. I know what I think I feel, but I have no idea what I'm going to feel like when we leave here, and neither does he. I also have a huge mess to look forward to when I get home. I have no right to expect him to want to muck out those stalls with me. That's not what he signed up for."

"I guess that remains to be seen. I've never known Galen to run from a little hard work." Cat eyed Lacey for a long moment before lugging her suitcase over to the dresser and unpacking. "I was going to ask if I should get another place to stay so you two could have some privacy, but there will be two solid doors between us, so that won't be an issue. Besides, that will give me the daytime hours to satisfy my nosiness and watch how you guys act around each other. This is too juicy to miss."

"We're not going to act like anything around each other." Now that Cat was here, everything was probably going to go right back to the way it was. He might not even want to share the bedroom with her anymore. She swallowed the bitter disappointment threatening to choke her. "I'm sure Galen and I will figure it out. No matter what, it will work out fine. Now let's stop talking about this. You came all the way here to be with me, and I love you for it, so what are we going to do on your first night in Puerto Rico?"

Cat seemed ready to press further, but mercifully, she let her off the hook. "Karaoke, maybe? Some dancing?"

"Sounds fun. We can hang at the beach for the day. Then I'll call the concierge and see where to go."

She was about to step out the door but Cat's voice stopped her. "I don't know whether it's the Puerto Rican air or my brother, but you've never looked better."

Lacey forced a smile and closed the door. Cat had always been perceptive, and today was no different. Now that it was right in her face, she had to accept the truth. Puerto Rico, while amazing, had next to nothing to do with her current state. It was Galen. He'd made her feel special and sexy and beautiful. And if that were the case, what would she feel like when he was out of her life again?

· · ·

Galen took a long swig from his beer bottle and watched his sister and her best friend on the dance floor, bopping around, singing along with an old Spice Girls tune. Lacey wore a short-sleeve blouse that hung off one newly browned shoulder and a pair of khaki shorts. Her beige high-heeled sandals made her already long legs look even longer, and he found himself wondering, not for the first time, if he'd ever get to feel those legs around him again now that Cat had shown up.

He loved his sister and under normal circumstances enjoyed hanging out with her now that they were grown. But he couldn't deny that when he'd walked out of the shower and saw her standing there, his stomach dropped. What a crappy brother. She'd probably thought she was doing him a favor by coming to take over aftercare for their ailing runaway bride. How could she know he was administering the antidote and enjoying every second of it?

At least, he had been right up until Lacey sent him that panicked look. The wild-eyed, *don't say anything* stare when he'd seen Cat. That shit hurt. If he'd been wondering what was going to happen between them once they left Puerto Rico, he needn't wonder any further. Clearly she planned to move on with her life, and their fling would be exactly that. A fling. One happy footnote to mark the end of her tragedy, not even worthy of explaining to her best friend.

He almost let her get away with it, but at the last second, he couldn't help himself. He'd thrown down the gauntlet to see if she would try to wriggle out of it or if she would own it. Own *him* and this thing between them. To his relief, she had. She'd been embarrassed but more for not telling his sister about them before than anything else. She certainly didn't seem angry at him, which was what he'd been expecting. Then she'd deflated him yet again with her insistence that this was a fling. Now he was fuck-all confused. Were they going to continue on with Cat there or were they calling it quits? He'd been banking on this week in hopes of convincing Lacey that they could have something more than just a fling. Now he might not even have that.

The song ended and he flagged down the waitress to order them another round.

The aging MC leaned into the mic. "Okay, ladies and gentlemen, this is going to be a fun one. We've got some new singers coming up here for you. Give it up for Cat and Lacey!"

The pair of them climbed the stage stairs and the beginning chords of "Two Princes" by the Spin Doctors began to play. Galen couldn't help but grin. He'd been forced to listen to this song on an endless loop when Cat and Lacey had discovered it almost two decades ago. This was going to be interesting.

Within the first two lines, as they traded back and forth with ease, never even glancing at the screen, it became clear that this song was a karaoke favorite of theirs. They hammed it up big and broke into interpretive dance at points. Galen couldn't keep his eyes off Lacey. Her shoulders shimmying, cheeks pink from laughing. Cat was a good influence on her. When they finished with a deep bow, the place exploded into applause. He stuck his pinkies into his mouth and whistled for good measure.

The girls smiled and waved, then leaped off the stage. The group of guys seated at the table in front of him was hooping and howling when the two women walked by. A dark-haired gym rat went in for a move.

"Great job, ladies." He held up a hand for high fives, which Lacey and Cat gave with matching grins.

A wiry blond guy from the group stood with his hand over his heart and spoke with a thick Boston accent. "If you were with me, I'd love you so hard, you wouldn't need two princes. I'd be your king and you'd be my queen." His line was laughably bad, but apparently the accent turning "hard" into "hahd" was enough to get their attention. He drew Cat and Lacey into a conversation about hometowns and New England.

The waitress returned with their drinks, and Galen uttered a perfunctory thanks. Blondie and his wingman were starting to get on his nerves now, lavishing Lacey and Cat with compliments. The next song had begun, so he had to inch closer to hear them.

"You are so beautiful, I swear. If I had a girl like you, I could die a happy man." This aimed at Lacey from Gym Rat.

She smiled politely, but then turned and caught Galen's eye. Was that a plea in her eyes or was it wishful thinking on his part? At the very least, she didn't want any PDA in front of Cat, or at least that's what it had seemed like back at the villa. But when Gym Rat closed a meaty paw on her shoulder, nothing short of a zombie apocalypse would have stopped him. Galen picked up the beer he'd ordered her and approached, slipping a possessive arm around her trim waist. "Hey, squirt. Nice job out there."

Lacey turned a grateful smile his way and accepted the bottle. "Thanks."

Gym Rat gave him the hard eye, and for a second Galen wondered if he was going to press his luck, but he backed off. "Hey buddy, how's it going?" he asked, releasing Lacey's shoulder.

"Pretty good, thanks."

Galen had obviously shat on their party plans because after an awkward minute of mostly silence, the Boston guys dispersed, making their way to the pool table.

"Thanks," Lacey said, the relief evident on her face. "I never quite know what to do in those situations."

"Well, don't expect me to thank you for cock-blocking me," Cat grumbled. "You come over here to pee on your girlfriend like some sort of lone wolf and you scared my prospect away with your macho display."

"I'm not his girlfriend," Lacey mumbled.

As if he needed the reminder. "She looked uncomfortable." He shrugged as if to say he'd do it for anybody.

"Whatever. Did you at least get me a drink?"

He jerked his chin toward the table where her mojito sat, and she grabbed it. "These things are too delicious, which could be a serious problem."

They paused to clap for the group of ladies who'd done a Sinatra song. When the applause died down, the MC bent toward the mic again. "Welcome back to the stage, Lacey, going solo this time!"

She turned a stricken gaze to Cat. "You didn't."

"Oh, but I did. Come on, I came all the way here to be

with you. The least you can do is sing my song."

Lacey groaned. "Stop with the guilt. It's not like you followed me to Siberia. We're in paradise, and you're getting a weeklong vacation. That doesn't mean you get to boss me for the next seven days."

"Who are you kidding? I boss you three hundred sixty-five days a year, and you love it. Now get your cute little ass up there and sing my song."

She sent a nervous glance at Galen and he tapped the tip of her nose with his finger. "You'll be great."

She took a long swallow of her beer, setting it down only when the MC started playfully chanting her name, which the crowd took up with glee.

"She's actually a fantastic singer," Cat said as they watched Lacey climb the stage stairs again. "I always have to go up with her at first to lube her up a little, but wait till you hear what she can do."

The strains of a familiar song by Heart made him smile. She, Becca, and Cat had put on a show for him and the rest of the family when they were in second grade. They'd danced and lip-synced to this song with spoons for microphones. Even then, Becca and Lacey had swayed in the background, chirping up during the chorus while Cat hogged the attention, strutting her stuff. He'd acted put upon and annoyed, as was required at that age, but they'd been pretty adorable.

Grown-up Lacey opened her mouth, and as a sweet, husky tone rang from her throat, the smile slid from his face. It was like a full-on body shot. A solid blow to the solar plexus that had him short of breath. She didn't just sing, she left it all out there, feeling every line…every word of it. When she sang about wanting and waiting, it was so real, it gave him chills. And when she claimed she never really cared until she met him, it felt like every word was *for* him. He managed to tear his gaze away for a second only to realize that every other guy in the place felt the same way he did.

Captivated.

During the guitar solo, Cat turned to grin at him. "And this, dear brother, is why we come to karaoke. It's the one place where she really lets it all out, you know?"

He nodded, still dazed.

His sister's face turned serious, and she closed a gentle hand over his forearm. "That look on her face when she sings? It's the same expression she gets when she talks about you. When we were getting ready to come here she was telling me about the boxing lessons, your almost-orgy, and all the fun stuff you've been doing. And she was…glowing." Cat's green gaze locked onto his with the intensity of a laser beam, and her grip tightened. "Do not fuck with her. She's fragile right now. I love you, but I will cut your heart out. Understand what I'm saying, bro?"

He nodded and tugged his arm from his sister's claw before she did some damage. "I hear you loud and clear."

He wondered if she'd given Lacey the same speech. Probably. But at the end of the day, it was Lacey and him who needed to figure out what, if anything, came next. His instinct was to push. He knew he wanted more time with her. He wasn't ready to let go yet. And if Cat's intuition was right, neither was Lacey. But she'd literally been a bride only a week ago. After what she'd been through, fragile was putting it mildly. Confused, scared, shocked, betrayed. She was a writhing mass of emotion when they'd first gotten to Puerto Rico. Just because she seemed okay now didn't mean there weren't deeper issues at play. Even if she did feel like this could be more than a fling, could her feelings even be trusted?

Rebound.

He'd tried to keep it at bay, but the term reared its ugly

head and burrowed its way further into his mind, digging its hooks deep. If he were on the outside looking in, he'd call it from a mile away. He'd say, "Don't get attached, man. You're the rebound guy." It didn't feel that way with Lacey, though. It felt real and right. Then again, what rebound guy ever knew he was the rebound guy until it was over and he was left standing there with his dick in his hand and a sleepy, confused smile on his face?

Fuck, he so didn't want that to be him.

The last note rang out and the audience went crazy, chanting her name and howling their approval. She picked her way through the crowd, stopping every few steps to give high fives to her new fans and politely shake her head—probably offers of drinks, though one appeared to be a proposal. She caught him staring and blushed, sending a beaming smile his way that warmed him clear through.

And just like that, it was decided. He might be the rebound guy right now, but there was no way he was going out like that. It was time to do what he did best.

Fight for what he wanted.

Chapter Ten

Lacey stared at the bedroom door, silently willing it to open. They'd gotten home from the karaoke bar a couple hours before, and Galen had been conspicuously absent since. He'd claimed he was "going out for a while," but she and Cat had watched almost all of *Good Will Hunting* and he still hadn't come back. Cat's head had started bobbing and she struggled to keep her eyes open, so Lacey had sent her to bed. She'd waited a few more minutes but finally followed suit, promising herself that she wouldn't wait up for him. The villa's front door had squealed open a little while later, but that was twenty minutes ago, and he still hadn't come into the bedroom.

She flicked off the light, forcing herself to stay in bed and not get up to grill him about where he'd gone. He was a big boy, and if he wanted to stay out all night, who was she to say anything?

No one. She had no claim on him at all.

She covered her face with the pillow and tried not to cry. He'd probably decided to sleep on the couch now that Cat was here. Whatever they'd had was over. She'd never get to kiss him again, or run her hands down the thick muscles in his back, or smell—

The sound of the doorknob turning sent her heart into overdrive. "Cat?" she called breathlessly. *Please don't be Cat, please don't be Cat.*

She tossed the pillow aside and squinted, straining to see the doorway in the darkness. It opened on a whisper, and a hulking silhouette filled the space. *Not Cat.*

"Did I wake you?" His voice was soft and gentle.

"No." She struggled to keep her tone even, not wanting to sound like a demanding harpy, despite the questions crowding her brain. *Where did you go? What did you do?* And most pathetic, *Do you still want me?* She bit her cheek to keep from crying.

"Sorry I took so long. I had to pick up a few things, and they were a little harder to locate than I had originally planned. The, ah, language barrier proved to be a problem. I was going to call Cat, but I left my phone in my other pants."

She didn't trust herself to speak without a telling crack, so she slid over to make room for him on the bed and hoped it would be answer enough.

"Nope. I need you to get up and come with me." He crossed the room and held out his hand.

"It's almost midnight," she said in halfhearted protest but gave him her hand. There was no question she would go. She just needed a second to recover from dizzy relief over his return.

"So it is. Are you going to turn into a pumpkin?"

She shook her head.

"Well then what are you waiting for? I promise to make it worth your while." The slow drawl was brimming with sensual promise. She shivered.

"Are we leaving the villa? Wh-what should I wear?"

"Whatever you have on is fine. We're not going far."

Her curiosity was piqued but nerves made her hesitate. If she didn't know where they were going or what they were doing, how could she mentally prepare? What if she might need something and she didn't bring it because he hadn't given her a chance to make a quick list? What if—

"Stop thinking, squirt. Feel for once." He bent low and scooped her into his arms. "Do you want to come…with me?" he whispered, his warm breath caressing her cheek.

His body was warm from the balmy night air, and she snuggled in closer. "Yes." *And it doesn't matter where*, she realized with a start. She would go anywhere if it meant another night in his arms.

Some of the tension seemed to drain out of him, and he dropped a kiss onto her forehead. "I'm so glad." He carried her through the villa to the French doors leading to the pool. "Can you get that?"

She pushed down the lever, and he toed the door open. When he stepped out to the tiny pool area, she gasped. The small round swimming pool was surrounded by dozens of flickering candles, and a bottle of wine sat in an ice-filled bucket next to the steps. A snowy white comforter littered with deep red pillows lay on the patio stones.

The whole time she'd been stewing over his absence, he'd been planning this romantic tryst. She blinked back hot tears.

"I know our pool isn't nearly as grand as Cyrus and Nikki's, but you seemed to really enjoy the water. I was thinking we could finish what we started at their house that night right here."

"Plus, you were afraid Cat would hear us in the other room." She met his gaze and offered a teasing grin.

"She wouldn't hear me. You're the screamer."

She started to protest when something next to the wine

bucket caught her eye. "What's that?"

He set her down and picked up the small wrapped box. "It's a surprise for a little later." The gleam in his eye set her heart thumping, and she resisted the urge to snatch it from him and look inside. "I know that look, control freak, but you're going to have to wait." He tucked a stray lock of hair behind her ear, and the tender expression on his face took the sting out of his words.

When he offered her wine, she nodded. He set the gift on the blanket and opened the bottle to pour them each a glass.

"To no regrets," he said, clinking his glass to hers.

She mimicked his toast before taking a sip. It was icy cold and sweetly tart, and she sighed with pleasure. "Nice."

He set down his glass and lifted a hand to the hem of his T-shirt, stripping it off and tossing it onto the chair behind him. After a week of seeing and touching him, she would have expected to have gotten over her initial obsession with his body, but that was far from the case. It was a jolt to her system every single time, and she drank in the sight, allowing her gaze to trip over his broad shoulders, down his chest, and past his sleek abs to the sexy smattering of hair leading to the button fly of his shorts. Shorts that were getting tighter right before her eyes. She dampened her lips, suddenly desperate to taste him there.

"When you look at me like that, I feel ten feet tall," he said softly.

Emotion clogged her throat, but she swallowed it back. "Women must look at you like that all the time."

"I'm not talking about what other women do. I'm talking about you and me." Those dark eyes were intense, as if he knew she was trying to keep her distance and wasn't going to allow it.

"You make me feel…special, too. It scares me."

"You should always feel special, whether I'm around or not."

She nodded, but inside she wanted to weep. When she tried to imagine what her days would be like without him, the sadness was unbearable.

"Are you going to get your skinny-dipping suit on or what? I'm not going to be the only one naked in the pool." He strode to the steps and stripped off his shorts, kicking them to the side.

Even more determined to live in the moment, she soaked in the view, envying his grace as he walked down the stairs into the clear blue water.

"Come on in, the water's fine," he called with a wicked grin.

She didn't hesitate. A few minutes earlier she hadn't even been sure she would get another chance to be with him and there was no way she was squandering it. She set down her glass and straightened to slip her tank top over her head. Next came the boxers, and then she faced him. His hum of appreciation echoed across the water, and she fought the urge to cover herself, forcing her fisted hands to drop to her sides.

"Damn, woman. Elle MacPherson's got nothing on you." He let out a long wolf whistle.

"Oh no? Well maybe you should have a poster of *me* over your bed, then."

"You give me a poster of you like that, babe, and I will hang it up in a heartbeat. In fact, I'll hang one in every room."

She stood a little straighter as the instinct to hide faded under the heat of his gaze. He held out a hand to her, and she stepped into the pool, murmuring with pleasure at the warm water caressing her ankles.

"Almost like a bath," she said, taking his hand. He led her down the rest of the stairs until she was waist deep, standing a scant few inches from him. She craned her neck to see his face. "What now, boss?" She couldn't keep the note of excitement from her voice as the water cradled her hypersensitive flesh intimately like an invisible hand.

"A massage."

Not what she'd expected, but she certainly wouldn't turn it down. "I'd love that."

He sat on one of the wide steps and pulled her down between his legs. With a sweep of his hand, he pushed her hair aside, leaving her back bare to his attention. He traced the line of her shoulders first, and she let her head fall forward to give him more room. She couldn't hold back the sigh at his gentle touch. He took his time, starting out soft and slow, drawing shapes on her back with his damp fingers, riding that sublime line between tickling her and making her squirm. Heat rushed to the spot between her thighs, and she wriggled against him until she could feel the weight of his sex, hot and heavy, branding her lower back.

"Mmm," she moaned. "This is lovely."

He dropped a sucking kiss to her nape and she shivered. Her breasts felt heavy and tight from the warm water lapping at her now hard nipples and she pressed back against Galen's hard chest, hoping his displaced hands would come around front to sooth the ache that was growing by leaps and bounds. His low, sexy laugh made her bold, and she pushed her bottom back hard until she was flush against his groin and his thighs hugged her hips tight.

"Tell me what you want, babe." His mouth was so close to her ear, the warm wash of his breath sent a tingle straight to her core.

"You. Inside me."

"You can count on it. But not yet." He flipped her around to face him, and she purred low in her throat as his stiff member pressed insistently at the juncture of her thighs. If she opened a little bit, she could—

"You naughty, naughty girl." He slid two hands down to cup her ass, holding her in place. "Naughty girls need to be punished, don't you think?" She was only half listening as she leaned forward to nip his chin. "Don't try to distract me. What do you think your punishment should be? A spanking?"

Her ears perked up then. "Well, I don't know about that," she said, and tried to climb off him. Her heart pounded with a healthy dose of fear mixed with a whole lot of something else just as scary.

"No? I think you'd be surprised to find you might like it." He held her tight and pursed his lips, as if deep in thought. "Maybe a tongue lashing, then?"

She stopped struggling and her clit pulsed in muscle memory. Like one of Pavlov's dogs, she was practically drooling at the thought of his mouth on her again.

His warm brown eyes danced, and he shook his head. "I guess that's out because you look more like I offered you a money tree than a punishment. A spanking it is."

He stood and lifted her with ease, in spite of her halfhearted struggles, and flipped her over his lap, securing her with one thick forearm. "Grip the side to brace yourself."

His gruff command sent her nerves into overdrive. "I don't know. I've never done anything like this before, and I'm not a huge fan of pain." The words had barely left her lips when he slipped his big palm over her ass and squeezed.

"Tell me no, then."

She couldn't make herself say it. As afraid as she was, she trusted him, and if he said she would like it—

"Ouch!" The sting when his palm connected with her wet cheek was sharp and instant. He was wrong. It frigging hurt. She opened her mouth to tell him to stop, but then his hand was on her, kneading the offended spot. She groaned and pressed harder into his lap, rewarded when his shaft nudged against her clit.

Another slap landed. "Mmph." This time, she didn't cry out, instead biting her lip through the sting. And again his magic hand was there, rubbing away the hurt while creating a dull ache between her thighs.

"Your ass makes me so fucking crazy. So round and sweet."

Smack.

This time, only a sigh escaped her when the sharp slap sent a bolt of heat straight between her thighs.

"Again," she whispered, crushing her hips against him now, seeking some relief for the grinding need that drove her.

"Oh, yeah." He swung again, this time switching cheeks, then rocking against her. He slipped the hand anchoring her around to caress her breast, tweaking the stiff nipple until she bucked against him. Right when she thought she might explode from sensory overload, his free hand slid down the crevice of her bottom, then lower still until he found her soaking wet slit.

He tested her with the tips of his fingers and she writhed against his hand, begging him without words for more.

"That's my girl," he ground out and plunged two fingers deep. Blood rushed to her ears and every nerve ending in her body went on high alert. One hand on her nipple, the sweet sting on her ass, the glide of his clever fingers, working her. She was so close…

"Jesus, Galen. You're going to make me come."

He pulled his hands away and cradled her to him, sucking in a few harsh breaths. "I want to be inside you. I need to feel that pussy squeezing my cock when you come." He slid her off his lap and led her back into the water toward the ledge of the pool. She turned to face him, but he held her in place.

"Face the fence," he said. The hunger in his voice sent a sizzle of anticipation down her spine. She rested her arms against the ledge and waited breathlessly for whatever came next. He wrapped his arms around her from behind to cup her breasts. He rolled the stiff peaks between his thumbs and forefingers and she arched against him.

"If you want to feel me come, you'd better saddle up, cowboy." She groaned, the rawness of her voice shocking her. She waited for the shame...but it never came.

He slipped his hands beneath the water, tugging her hips backward so that she was bent at an angle, and spread her thighs. He raked his hands down her back, allowing them to drift lower, palming her ass and finally reaching her center. He drove one thick finger deep, sliding in and out, then added a second until she cried out. The need to come bore down on her like a locomotive and her legs shook.

"Now. God, please now." She leaned forward, draping her arms over the cool marble ledge, desperate for something, anything to stop the exquisite agony and topple her over the razor's edge.

"Move over. A little to the left."

He closed a hand on her hip and guided her over a foot, then two. A rush of water blasted against her hip and then... *there. Right there.* The jet pulsed against her, lapping at her swollen flesh and she bucked, groaning.

Galen was there, crooning words of praise in her ear, clutching at her hips, ready to finish her. He pressed forward, sliding into her in one mighty thrust. The water pulsed relentlessly against her and she froze, overwhelmed by the sensation.

"I wish you could see what I see. My cock slipping in and out of those sweet pink folds." His husky voice grounded her, and she pushed back against him, taking him deeper in a counter thrust. "Damn it, Lacey, I can't hold back if you do that."

"Don't hold back. Please, don't hold back," she pleaded.

The dam broke. He gripped her hips tighter and began to fuck her in earnest. Long, sure strokes, every one of which sent the head of his cock dragging against some magical place deep, deep inside her that left her sobbing. He pushed her forward until the jet was only a few inches away and the water went from a low pulse to a pressured spurt against the sensitive knot between her legs. Then she was flying.

"Galen!"

Her muscles strained as the orgasm broke over her. A keening wail rose in her throat and he pounded into her, filling her to bursting. Galen tensed behind her and growled, his hands digging into her hips. He leaned forward to sink his teeth into her shoulder, muffling his shout of completion as he pulsed inside her.

For an endless moment they stayed locked in their embrace until he drew her away from the jets that were far too powerful for her now sensitive flesh.

"Pools rock," she murmured. He was slumped over her, stroking her rib cage lazily and she could feel his heart still pounding against her back.

He nodded. "Totally."

He swept her hair to the side and pressed a kiss to the back of her neck. The simple show of affection sent her emotions tilting out of control. She'd never felt this way before, and it left her reeling. It took all the effort she could muster to swallow the words burning on her lips.

Stay with me.

• • •

Galen stared at the ceiling, replaying the night's highlights in his mind. That had been hands down the best sex of his life, and he didn't have a clue what to do about it. He didn't want to pressure her, but he was quickly getting to the point that the idea of a brief fling didn't sit well at all anymore.

Lacey shifted in his arms with a sleepy murmur, and he pulled her closer, tucking her tighter against his chest. He fingered the gold chain against her neck and smiled. She'd looked really pleased when he gave it to her. That had to be a good sign, didn't it?

They'd finished making love in the pool and had moved to lie on the blanket and enjoy the bottle of wine when the package had caught her eye again. "Go ahead, open it," he'd urged.

She tore the paper off like a kid at Christmas. Nestled inside the box was a slim gold chain with a boxing glove charm. She pulled it out immediately and handed it to him. "Put it on me."

He hooked it around her neck and she turned so he could see. "Looks great. Do you know why I got that for you?"

"Because you're a fighter."

"No, because you are. I don't ever want you to forget that, or how strong you are."

Her eyes had gotten suspiciously shiny, and she went quiet for a long moment before she took his hand. "This is the best gift I've ever gotten, Galen. Thank you."

Now, with her soft snore tickling his chest, he wondered if his eyes were a little shiny, too. He knew one thing for sure, though. A woman didn't look at a rebound guy that way. Tonight, Lacey had been 100 percent, unequivocally his. Now he just had to figure out how to keep her.

Chapter Eleven

"What in God's name is going on here?"

Lacey's eyes sprang open as she was awakened from a dead sleep. Horror drenched her when she registered the sound of her mother's voice. Rowena Garrity stood with her arms folded over her chest, her back ramrod straight, stormy gray eyes filled with accusations.

"Mother? Wh-what are you doing here?" She pulled away from a groggy and confused Galen to drag the sheets up to her neck for more cover. Luckily, he had gotten up for a snack in the middle of the night and was only half naked. Too bad the same couldn't be said for her.

"I'm so sorry, Lace." Cat stepped in behind Rowena, her cheeks flushed with anger. "She caught me on the way back up from breakfast. I told her she should call first, but, well…" Cat's disgusted face said it all. Rowena was like a titanium tank. If she wanted in, there was no stopping her.

"It's okay, Cat. You're not in the wrong here. Mother, what's going on?"

"I believe that is the question you should be answering." In spite of the frost in her tone, true to form, Rowena never raised her voice. She turned her bone-chilling gaze on Galen. He sat up, but to his credit, he didn't flinch. Or explode into flames. "And you? I would say I expected better, but then we both know that would be a lie. I'd appreciate it if you'd give me some time to speak with my daughter, Mr. Thomas." She turned to face Cat and dismissed her with a nod. "Mary Catherine."

Galen's face was stony. "Ma'am, I'm happy to do whatever makes Lacey comfortable, and if she'd like me to stay, then that's what I'll be doing."

"From where I'm standing it appears you've done enough already. Taking advantage of a heartbroken young woman so you could get into her bed after her marriage implodes hardly seems like the act of someone concerned with my daughter's happiness. She's in no state to make decisions, and you took advantage like a carrion-feeder."

Lacey's whole body shook, but she managed to keep her tone even. "I'm sorry, Galen. You shouldn't have to listen to this. It's better if I deal with her on my own. You don't have to leave, though—we will. Mother, please wait out front. I'll change and meet you down the path at the café. We can talk there."

"It was bad enough I had to confide in the staff with those archaic notes, which incidentally, I'm furious at you for disregarding. Now you think I want to discuss your infidelity in public?" Her mouth flattened into an angry slash of red against her ivory complexion.

"Infidelity?" The tenuous hold she had over her emotions threatened to snap, but she hung strong. "After what he did, I hardly owe him any loyalty."

"Of course you do. We had an agreement, and Garritys always meet their obligations." She hitched her Chanel bag higher onto her shoulder and waved an imperious hand in

Lacey's direction. "Get a move on. We need to hash this out ASAP so we can put this ridiculousness behind us. I swear, I don't know what you were thinking. You're a married woman, for the love of God. Unacceptable."

Lacey sat straighter, anger handily defeating the initial humiliation of having her mother find her *in flagrante delicto*. "Don't throw that in my face. You know perfectly well the paperwork was never filed."

Galen took her hand and gave it a reassuring squeeze. Rowena narrowed her steely gaze. "Semantics. You made vows. Moreover, we signed contracts."

Lacey allowed herself a short, harsh laugh. "Vows? Those were broken the minute I walked in on him with Becca. As for the merger, that has nothing to do with me. I told Dad to go ahead with it. This is my issue and my life."

"Well, your father has all of a sudden decided that continuing after Marty hurt you like that would be a betrayal. As a display of his support, he's decided that the merger is off. If you can't forgive Marty, neither can he. That's why you need to come home and give this marriage a chance, Lacey."

"I hope you're not suggesting that I spend the rest of my life with a man who was unfaithful to me and who I no longer hold any affection for in order for your business to prosper financially."

"*Our* business," her mother corrected coolly. "The last time I checked, you were a Garrity as well. And I refuse to air out any more of our family issues in front of *these* people. Meet me at the café in the main hall in fifteen minutes. I'll get us a quiet corner, and we can deal with this like grown-ups." She turned on her tasteful spindly heel and swept out of the room without waiting for an answer.

These people. As if they were some subhuman race. Lacey stared at the open door for a long moment, still reeling from the shock. She'd gone to sleep feeling happy and safe and satisfied and had woken up to a nightmare.

"Well, that was awkward," Cat said, stepping back into the room. Her expressive face was high with color, and Lacey knew it had taken every ounce of her friend's self-control not to tell Rowena where to go. Despite her mother's best efforts to get Cat to behave like the low-class broad she'd determined her to be, Cat had always managed to handle herself beautifully. In the past twenty years, she'd never once told Rowena what she really thought of her. By now, she seemed mostly immune to Lacey's mother's cold but polite forbearance capped by random, subtle putdowns. But Galen wasn't used to it, and Lacey could feel the tension pouring off him.

"I'm so sorry, you guys. She has no right to treat you that way. I know she's a nightmare. Let me get this over with. I'll talk to her and send her on her way."

Galen released her hand and nodded. "You do what you need to." In spite of his words, she could feel the change in him. It was like he'd erected a wall between them in just a few short minutes, and she hated it.

"I won't be long. Then we can go fishing like we'd planned, all right?" She despised the pleading tone of her voice but couldn't seem to help it. "It will be fine, you'll see."

Galen nodded and rolled to his feet. "Sure thing."

Cat scowled at him. "Don't let her get in your head, Lace. Stay strong. We'll be here when you get back. Come on, bro, let's go for a swim and let her get ready."

They left Lacey alone in the bed. Their bed. The look on Galen's face had about done her in, and she wanted nothing more than to rail at her mother for her behavior. The thought got her up and moving, fueled by her anger. It was time to put her mother on notice. She wasn't the same woman she used to be before her wedding day. Before Puerto Rico. Before Galen.

And more than that? She wasn't going back.

Less than twenty minutes later, she stood at the entrance to the café. Sucking in a deep breath, she yanked open the door and stepped inside.

Her mother was already seated, and the hostess led Lacey to the small booth in the farthest corner where Rowena sat with a glass of grapefruit juice and a face just as sour.

She glanced pointedly at the slim gold watch on her wrist, but Lacey didn't bite. She slid onto the booth and faced Rowena head-on. "I don't appreciate the way you treated my friends."

"And I don't appreciate your tone or the way you're behaving. I think it's time for you to look a little harder at the people you call friends." Her mother plucked up the napkin in front of her, opened it with a *snap*, and settled it on her lap before meeting Lacey's gaze again. "A girl who drags you into trouble by the nose since childhood fixes you up with her brute of a brother." Her voice had risen slightly and a blue vein throbbed behind the thin skin of her forehead. She stilled, took a breath, and folded her hands primly on the table, modulating her tone again. "A brother who pretends to be a gallant rescuer of runaway brides, only to sweep you off to Puerto Rico and take advantage of your vulnerability and wealth. And they should have my respect?"

"No. No, don't you make it sound like that. Every time something doesn't go exactly the way you want it to, you start this bull. The manipulation and bending the truth, putting a nefarious spin on everything. Cat is like a sister to me. She's been nothing but good for me, and Galen came here and helped me through a very rough time. I didn't pay for his ticket, and he has his own money. They are the best friends

I've ever had."

"Well then I suggest you start interviewing for new ones, because a true friend wouldn't lead you down a path of destruction and heartache or be party to the breakup of your marriage."

"I. Am. Not. Married." She all but spat the words, but her mother barely blinked.

The determination in Rowena's eyes was chilling. "You spoke vows. We had a contract with Marty's family. The merger is in place. We have made promises to clients about this expansion; there are deals on the table contingent on this going through. This isn't some child's game to be tossed aside over a crush. People's livelihoods depend on this. Already the negative press is damaging our name. We need to make this right, and we need to do it now."

It took every ounce of self-discipline to keep her voice low enough that the other diners wouldn't hear. "You know, Mother, people who negotiate these types of arrangements have a name. They're called Madames. Or pimps, if you prefer."

Rowena didn't bother to feign shock or horror. Instead, her shrewd eyes narrowed at the barb. She looked like a snake. "Don't be such a drama queen. I'm not selling you off to some lecherous sheik. Marty is a nice young man with an impeccable pedigree. Our families are doing what good families have done for generations. Ensuring that our son and daughter settle down with a spouse of equal standing."

"And in your estimation"—she could feel the pulse throbbing in her temple and fought to keep her composure—"a man who would cheat on his wedding day is my equal?"

Her mother shrugged her slim shoulders and took a sip of juice before responding. "I'm speaking socially. You thought he was fine until his little slip. In fact, you were happy to marry him. As for the man's character, it's no worse than most. You always were such a little prude about that. Men are lustful beasts, Lacey. Make your home, make your babies, spend his money, enjoy the club and your social life, and turn the other cheek to the rest of it."

Lacey drew back, as much stunned that her mother still had the ability to shock her as she was by her words. "You can't possibly believe that."

"Oh, but I do."

"I guess that's easy to say, since Dad never cheated. Why you would want that for your only daughter, I don't—"

Rowena's mirthless, tinkling laugh skated down Lacey's spine like an icicle. "Oh, darling girl, don't be so naive. How do you think I got him to buy me the house in the Hamptons? Or that Bentley? Or this bracelet, for that matter." She held out her hand to examine the diamond bangle with a fond smile.

Lacey's stomach heaved, and she bit down on her trembling lip. Her mother had always been a dragon, but her father? A distant but doting teddy bear of a man. The one she could count on for a hug or an ear to bend when he was home to give it.

A cheater.

As much as she didn't want to believe it, when her mother met her gaze again, she saw the truth there, laid bare. She shook her head violently. "No. Not me. I don't want that. I won't have that. I want someone who will be honest and loyal and who loves me more than anything else in the world."

Rowena swept a hand over her flawless updo. "Then get a dog."

Lacey wouldn't give her the satisfaction of flinching. "I won't let you crush this dream for me."

"Is that what you think you have in your boxer up there? A dream?"

Lacey looked away, refusing to answer.

"Here's a wake-up call for you, then. If a vapid little man like Marty would cheat, why would you think one woman would be enough for your virile Mr. Thomas?"

Rowena's aim was true, and the venom-tipped arrow struck home. In spite of Lacey's immediate denial, she could already feel the insidious effects of the poison infiltrating her thoughts, seeping into her heart. Hadn't she thought that same thing herself? Hearing her mother reaffirm it made her ill, and every bit of confidence she'd gained since she'd gotten to Puerto Rico drained out of her. What would make her think she could possibly hold a man like Galen when she hadn't even managed to keep Marty interested long enough? When Marty had cheated, she'd been horrified, furious, and embarrassed. One thing she knew for sure. If she and Galen exchanged vows and then he was unfaithful?

It would break her.

She thought back to their magical night before and resisted the urge to tug at the chain hidden beneath her collar. She'd been so touched by his gift and the meaning behind it, but now she wondered if he'd been preparing her for his eventual departure from her life. All the speeches about her being strong and feeling special whether he was around or not...had he been telling her not to get too comfortable?

She shoved the nauseating thought away as the waitress came by to take their order. Rowena waved her off and when she left, her mother leaned forward, eyes softening a little. "I know I seem harsh sometimes. We both know I wasn't born with that coddling gene that so many women have. But I care for you a great deal, and as much as I'd like for the merger to go through, I'm also looking out for your best interests. And believe me, darling, it's in your best interest to marry a wealthy, pliable man and make your own happiness in this world. Men like Galen are nothing but heartache." Something flickered across her face. Regret?

The truth was suddenly so clear. "Who was he, Mother?"

"Excuse me?" Her smooth brow wrinkled in faux confusion, but the pain in her eyes sealed it.

"The man who hurt you. Who was it? Was it Dad or someone before him?" Lacey pressed. She reached out and took her mother's hand and for a split, heartrending second, she thought they might have some sort of breakthrough, a moment of honest emotion between them.

Maybe Rowena thought so, too, because she sat back, extricating herself from Lacey's grasp. "Spare me the melodrama," she said with a sniff. "This isn't some episode of *Dr. Phil*. I'm trying to remind you to be pragmatic. That was never a problem for you until your father insisted it wouldn't do any harm for you to hang around with the Thomas children."

Lacey hissed out a breath and tamped down her disappointment. She'd try reasoning with her one last time, and if that didn't work, she was done. "Cat and I have been friends since forever. I know you'd like to blame her for every little imagined misstep in my life, but she's the one person I know I can turn to for anything. And Galen didn't make me run away from my reception. That was all Marty's doing. In fact, I don't even know why you've come. Surely Marty accepts the fact that this situation is beyond repair. He's probably relieved that he and Becca can go public now."

Funny how that thought didn't even faze her. Galen was right. The two of them deserved each other, and if they managed to find happiness together, more power to them.

"Decidedly not. Marty recognized his mistake that very night and has been almost inconsolable. He desperately wants to reconcile with you. It was only my insistence that you needed some space that kept him from accompanying me here to win you back." Rowena opened her purse and pulled out a folded sheet of paper. "This is for you. I've already spoken to your husband. He's willing to overlook your abandonment and even the fact that you were here with another man to honor the agreement the two of you made. I expect no less of you."

Lacey gaped at the marriage certificate in shock. "Where did you get that? Fitz was going to destroy it."

"When he contacted Marty to let him know of his intention, Marty asked me to intervene. I called Ellory Fitzhume, and she was able to get the document from Allen."

Fitz, you damned turncoat. "You had no right to do that."

"It was for your own good. You're not thinking clearly and none of us want to see you act more rashly than you already have. Come home. Think it over for a week or so, away from the garish lights and nights of debauchery, and you'll see. This is all a mirage. If I'm wrong, then feel free to pick up with your boxer where you left off. If he actually cares, a few days won't make any difference, will it?"

She stood and dropped a twenty dollar bill on the table. "I'll be at the El San Juan Resort tonight. My flight leaves first thing in the morning, and I've purchased a second first-class ticket in your name so that you can join me. Take the night to say your good-byes, then come home so we can deal with this situation as delicately as possible and try to salvage this merger. There's nothing left for you here, Lacey."

She strode out of the restaurant without a backward glance. Lacey stared after her for a long moment, grief and fear rendering her immobile. And then she heard the sound of Galen's voice in her head.

You're a fighter. You're stronger than you know, squirt.

She fingered the glove around her neck and stood. Screw

Rowena. She was nothing but a lonely, bitter woman who had to control everyone and everything around her. Well, not anymore. Not with Lacey. She'd go back home when she was ready and not before.

She strode toward the exit, more than ready to get back to the villa. And back to Galen.

Chapter Twelve

"She'll be here any minute," Cat said, wringing her hands together. "Please, don't do this to her. At least wait to say good-bye."

Galen jammed another fistful of clothes into his suitcase. "I'm not doing anything to her. I'm doing it *for* her. Her mother is a witch, but she's also right about one thing. Lacey doesn't know what she really wants. Everything she's done has been because I pushed for it."

Fate was an evil bitch. After the single best night of his life, She'd snatched it all away with one of the worst mornings he could remember. Lacey's mother walking in and giving Lacey hell had been bad enough. But realizing that the witch had a point? It was killing him.

"She's pretty smart, bro. I think she'd know it if you manipulated her in some way."

"You're wrong. People never know it until it's too late. Even now my being here is going to sway her. She'll have her mom tugging her one way and me the other. I don't want to put her through that. She's dealt with enough, and she needs time to be alone and think about what she really wants." He scooped up the toiletries from the dresser and stuffed them into his bag. "Besides, we never talked about the future. I don't know if she even wants to be with me once we leave here, and it will only make it harder on both of us if I stay."

Cat snorted. "She wouldn't have slept with you if she wasn't already in love with you. She's not built that way."

"Caring about someone and wanting to build a future with him isn't the same thing at all. This is a decision Lacey needs to make on her own, without me distracting her. I hate to admit it, but I was wrong. I should have—" He ran a hand through his hair and growled. "I don't know, been here and supported her without any of the other stuff. Then, later down the line, if she felt the same way I did, we could have tried it then. The way things went down? It wasn't fair to her. I have more experience, and I definitely used it to my advantage."

He zipped up his bag and set it next to the door, which swung open a second later. His heart sank as Lacey's accusing gaze drilled into him.

"W-where are you going?"

Cat slipped out, giving Lacey's shoulder a gentle squeeze as she passed.

Lacey closed the door, squaring off with him. "I asked you a question."

Her voice quavered, and it was like sucker punch. He wanted nothing more than to walk over and hold her until that quaver went away. "I'm going back home."

She closed her eyes and seemed to collapse in on herself. "Why?" she croaked.

"Because you don't need me here fucking with your head. Your mom was right. You need some time alone to think about what you want."

The beat of hesitation was like a hot knife in the gut but at the same time, it strengthened his resolve.

"I want you," she finally whispered.

"You think that now." He didn't want to continue, hated driving her away when he wanted nothing more than to grab her and hang on tight, but he forced the words out. "I'm the polar opposite of the man who broke your heart. We've been on a whirlwind trip to paradise where it was my goal to make you come harder than you ever have, to take you places you'd never been before. Where I set out to blow your mind over and over until you couldn't remember what it was like to have another man's mouth on you. Where I encouraged you to be wild and free and to let yourself go. Who wouldn't love that? Especially after the hit your ego had taken.

"I didn't mean to, but fuck, Lacey. I *did* take advantage of you. And I'm not going to keep doing it. Maybe all I was ever meant to be was the rebound guy for you. If so, the job is done. You're going to be fine without Marty."

The tears streamed freely down her face now, and his throat tightened.

"And if not, if you decide—" He stopped short.

He couldn't tell her the whole of it. That he would be waiting for her, however long it took. That if she thought about it for a while and realized he wasn't the rebound guy, if she chose to be with him for the long haul, he would welcome her with open arms. That he fucking loved her. He totally fucking loved her. At some point, Little Lacey Garrity had delivered the haymaker and Whalin' Galen Thomas was down for the count. But saying those things out loud would be no less manipulative than what he'd done to that point. If she truly wanted to be with him, they would have a lifetime to make promises.

The thought gave him the strength he needed to pick up his bag. "No matter what, squirt, I have no regrets."

He bent low to press a kiss to her wet cheek and walked

out the door, a small, stubborn part of his heart hoping she would stop him, reassure him that everything they'd felt was real.

His heart broke a little more when she didn't.

• • •

Lacey stared blankly at the data running down the screen of her monitor, waiting to feel something. Anything. The success of their latest marketing campaign should have made her happy or at least given her a sense of satisfaction at a job well done. Instead she felt empty. Hollow.

She turned away from the screen with a sigh. It had been almost a month since she left Puerto Rico, and she was no closer to getting over Galen than she had been the day he'd left. Letting him walk out that door had been the hardest thing she'd ever done. Her stomach clenched from the memory, the moment that was a thousand times worse than finding Marty with Becca. But with her mother's hurtful words still ringing in her ears, she hadn't been able to bring herself to chase him when he'd walked away so easily. Maybe he'd been looking for a way out anyway. Rowena had given him that, and then some.

The first couple weeks, she'd waited for him to change his mind. To do something to indicate that he missed her as much as she missed him. Every time the phone rang, her heart stuttered. But as each day passed, hope faded a little more, and she knew he wasn't going to call. This time, when her office phone rang, she picked it up without even looking at the caller ID. "Lacey Garrity."

"Will you please meet me for lunch?" Cat's voice was filled with desperation.

Lacey winced. She'd been putting her friend off for

weeks now in hopes of hiding exactly how devastated she was by what had happened between Galen and her. The past few calls had been increasingly more insistent, but still she hedged. It wouldn't be fair to put her in the middle, and the last thing she needed was for Cat to see that she wasn't anywhere near getting over her brother. Especially since Galen had so clearly moved on. Just the other night there had been an announcement on ESPN about him challenging Manny Hermosa to a rematch for the belt. Once the money men hammered out a deal—and according to the buzz, they were very close to doing so—it would only be a few weeks before Galen would leave for Chicago to start training.

"I'm not asking again, Lace. If you say no, I'm going to sit in front of your house until you agree to talk to me. You're really scaring me."

"I don't mean to. I've been busy. It took a week to untangle the financial mess and send the gifts back to everyone who'd mailed them, then another to talk my mother off the ledge. She's finally come to terms with the fact that I'm not marrying Marty, but she's no longer speaking with me and is in full dragon mode with everyone else."

"I want to hear all about it. You can fill me in on everything over lunch."

This time, it wasn't a question. Lacey sighed. She had enough experience to recognize Cat on a mission. "Okay. Where do you want to go?"

"Alistair's, noon."

Lacey put the receiver back on the hook and gazed glumly out the window. April showers hadn't brought May flowers, they'd only brought more rain, which was fine by her. Sunshine and flowers only made her think of Puerto Rico. If she closed her eyes, she could almost hear the coquí frogs.

"Cut it out," she muttered to herself, and turned her

attention back to the numbers. Time healed all wounds, and soon she'd be okay again. At this rate, it would only take another twenty years or so.

The rest of the morning passed in a blur of phone calls and meetings and by the time noon came, she was grateful for the reprieve despite having to deal with the upcoming inquisition. Truth was, she'd hated blowing off Cat, and a part of her was glad her friend had forced her hand. It was bad enough without Galen, but not having Cat to lean on during such an emotional time had made it even harder.

By the time she got to Alistair's, Cat was already at a table sipping a glass of wine. "Want one?"

Lacey shook her head. "I have to go back to work. Don't you?"

"Nope. I cut out early. I'm going to the shore for the weekend with Steve."

"Who's Steve?"

"The new guy I've been seeing. See?" She glared at Lacey accusingly. "You've been avoiding me so hard, you don't even know about my boyfriend, Steve."

"You've called me, like, every other day! Just because we haven't gone out in a few weeks doesn't mean I'm avoiding you."

Her green eyes narrowed, and Lacey squirmed under the weight of her gaze. "You are a terrible liar. Always have been. Now what the fuck is going on with you? I've tried to give you time and space to take care of your business like Galen asked me to, but this is getting out of control. Why haven't you called him?" Cat tapped her manicured purple nails on the tabletop impatiently.

Lacey swallowed the knot lodged in her throat and strived for a normal tone. "I don't even have his number." She barked out a harsh laugh. "How telling is that? We weren't boyfriend and girlfriend. It was a fling. A—"

"Bullshit. You're crazy about him. And he's damn sure crazy about you. He's been a miserable prick since you dumped him. I promised I would mind my own business. I swore I wouldn't get involved, but damn it, you two are screwing this all up."

Lacey speared a hand through her red curls and tugged like she was ready to pull them out. "You ever watch a movie with a group of attractive teenagers on a camping trip in a remote area, and two of them walk off to drink beer and do dirty things to each other, and you know the ax murderer is going to come and hack them up, but you can't say anything because they're on the big screen? That's what this is like. I know the ending to the story, and I know it could be different if you guys want it to be."

"First off, *he* dumped *me*, and he sure didn't look miserable on TV the other night when they interviewed him."

"Don't confuse how he behaves in an interview with real life. It's his job to swagger in, show confidence, and talk enough smack to get his potential opponent to pay attention. You know that as well as I do. You let him go. A word would have stopped him, Lacey. Surely you know that. Hell, I only saw how he looked when he was packing to leave, and *I* knew that. He's a wreck, and I know that because I go by his house every night to make sure he's eating."

Lacey's mouth went dry, and her pulse careened out of control. "Because of me?"

"Why else? He won't talk about it. Keeps telling me that he's fine, but I'm not stupid."

"So he didn't actually say it, then?"

"No. But I know for sure."

The hope that had sprung to life only a few seconds before died. "Cat, it could be a million things bothering him.

His career is winding down; maybe he's nervous about the fight or worried about what comes next."

"Watching the two people I love most hurting each other like this is killing me. Please. Go talk to him. I know he wants—"

Lacey held up a hand and willed herself not to cry. "Stop. You don't know. You want that to be the reason because it pushes all your romantic buttons to think about us pining away for each other after our wild week together and because you want to see us both happy. But I can't do it, Cat. I can't risk getting hurt again. Not right now."

"When, then? What happened to no regrets, Lace? You were different in Puerto Rico. I thought it changed you, but now, weeks later, everything is the same. Same job you couldn't care less about. Same relationship with The Admiral, same Lacey, afraid to live. Afraid to jump, in case she might fall."

The words rained on Lacey like blows, and she sat back, stunned. Her first instinct was to walk away. Hide her head under a blanket and lick her wounds. But white-hot anger came and displaced the hurt. "You have a lot of nerve. I had to deal with my mother my whole life and had a father who was hardly ever there. You've got two wonderful parents who think the sun rises and sets with you. It's a lot easier to jump when you know someone will be there to catch you if you fall, or at the very least be there with a bandage and a kiss. I never had that, so don't talk to me about tough." She snatched up Cat's wineglass and took a gulp before slamming it back onto the table. "And I quit my job, so there. I have another week before my replacement starts."

Cat's face split into a grin. "Awesome. That's what I want to see from you. Some fire. Fight. Stand up for who you want to be and what you want in your life. If that includes my brother, then you need to put on your big-girl pants and go get him."

The anger faded as quickly as it had come, and Lacey slumped in her chair. In spite of her methods, Cat was only trying to help. She met her friend's gaze. "What if I go talk to him and he doesn't want me?" she whispered. "Or what if he thinks he does and then later...what if my mother was right? What if I can't hold a man like Galen?"

"If he doesn't want you, he's a fool. And The Admiral has some screws loose. She doesn't know my brother from Adam. There is no one more loyal or dependable than Galen, and you are funny, and smart, and beautiful. You're everything a man like my brother could ever want. Stop making excuses because you're afraid. You have to do this because then at least you can say that you tried. Ten years from now if you're saddled with some balding Marty-type snoozer, you won't be left wondering what if and daydreaming about a time machine so you could come back to this day and have a do-over."

Lacey let her friend's words sink in. Could she stand it? If he came right out and said he didn't want to be with her, would she ever be okay again? She dug deep for the answer but came up empty. What she did know was that she'd let him walk away once and she'd never be okay if she didn't at least try to get him back.

"Where is he?"

Cat checked her watch and smiled. "Funny you should ask."

Chapter Thirteen

At first, Lacey's heart had almost leaped out of her chest. She was sure Galen was going to walk through the door, but instead Cat had thrown some bills on the table and dragged her out of the restaurant. Fifteen minutes later, they pulled up to Beazley's Gym on South Seventh Street. The parking lot was packed with both cars and news vans.

Lacey turned to Cat. "What's going on? You said he was at the gym, but what's all this stuff?"

"He *is* at the gym. Manny has accepted the terms for the rematch. Galen and his trainer are holding a press conference," Cat said, as casually as if she were announcing what she'd had for breakfast. She opened her door and swung her legs out.

Panic rose in Lacey's chest and hysterical laughter built in her throat. She opened her mouth to speak, and it bubbled over. Cat whipped around to face her with a baffled glare. "What is so funny?"

Lacey tried to talk, but the laughter kept coming, swiftly joined by tears. Her emotions were all over the place and she was pretty sure she was having a panic attack. She bent low and pressed her head between her knees.

"Okay, whoa. This was obviously a bad idea. You're in super crazy-pants mode right now." She pulled her legs back into the car and shut the door. "Let's go. We can just watch the press conference on TV and you can catch him later tonight when you've had a chance to think. Maybe make a pros and cons list."

That would be the safest thing to do. She'd had her fill of humiliation for the year, and the prospect of Galen denying her in front of a roomful of people made her legs feel jiggly. A sense of calm flowed over her and the laughter stopped. "No. I'm doing this. It's time for me to grow some balls. I've got to become the meat in my own sandwich now, you know?"

Cat turned and gave her a puzzled stare.

"What I mean is that I need to take control of my life and do what makes me happy. I'm fighting for what I want and I'm not going to play it safe this time in case I lose. I'm going to go big or go home. No more jabs for Lacey Garrity. I'm throwing the haymaker." Her chest went tight and she opened her car door. Despite the bravado, her gut churned. The thought of going back to life before Galen was too sad to bear.

She stepped out of the car and crossed the parking lot, her friend at her side. When they reached the door, it seemed larger than life. Somehow, if lions had flanked it, they wouldn't have seemed out of place. She pushed away the ludicrous thought and raised a hand to push it open.

A bald, hulking man in a suit standing next to the door held up a hand. "Press only."

Cat held up two red badges. "Family."

The behemoth nodded his shiny head and waved them in.

"Does he know I'm coming?" she whispered.

Cat didn't turn around, elbowing her way through the milling crowd of reporters. "Nope. Hell, I wasn't even sure you *were* coming."

"So where'd you get the second badge?"

"It's my mom's. She, uh, sort of knows what's going on and wanted you to have it. Just in case."

Lacey groaned. "No pressure."

"There isn't. Be honest, say what you came to say, and that's all you can do."

Lacey was scanning the room for some sign of Galen when a voice boomed over the portable speakers scattered around the perimeter. "All right, everyone. If you could take a seat, we'll start now. Galen, Max, and I will give our statements, and then we'll open the floor for Q and A."

Cat tugged Lacey over to the back row of chairs and they sat. It was only when the people in front of her did as well that she caught sight of Galen. He looked gorgeous, dressed in a white button-down shirt and tie. His tan had faded, the scruff on his chin was a little scruffier than usual, and his eyes looked tired, but to her, he was perfection.

For the first twenty minutes, the men took turns talking about the upcoming fight, talking about Manny Hermosa and about the things Galen was going to do differently to make sure he logged the win this time around. Lacey tried to focus but found herself lost staring at Galen.

It felt like hours by the time Max said, "Questions from the press?"

Lacey jerked, the words jarring her from her trance, and Cat gave her leg a reassuring squeeze.

A reporter in a brown ball cap stood. "Yes. Whalin', if you lose to Hermosa again, will you still consider retirement without the belt?"

"That's a good question. There's no way I'm losing this fight. I out-boxed him last time, and I'll out-box him again. But on the off chance that things don't fall my way, I will still retire. The outcome of the fight has no bearing on my decision.

Next?" He searched the room and for a second she was sure he would see her in the crowd but a slim female reporter in the far corner called out.

"Max, what kind of shape is Galen in after his last fight? Is eight months long enough to recover and train?"

"He only went five rounds, and he's in the best shape of his life. He's going to be more than ready, ain't that right, kid?" Max patted Galen on the arm and Galen nodded.

"Absolutely. Moore was fast, but he didn't land too many punches. I feel great, and I'm looking forward to hitting the gym super hard in the coming months."

Galen's manager held out a hand. "Anyone else?"

It was now or never. Lacey stood on jelly-legs and raised a trembling hand. "I have one."

Galen's gaze shot to hers and his eyes widened. "Lacey? What are you doing here?"

The people around her began to murmur, all turning in their seats to get a look at who was speaking. It took everything she had not to turn tail and run, but she met his gaze head-on. "I came to ask you a question."

Max leaned into his mic, his bristly black mustache making a crunching sound when he pressed his mouth too close. "Young lady, I'm afraid this session is only for members of the press."

Galen tapped Max on the arm. "It's okay, I got this one." His eyes were full of questions and Lacey swallowed hard.

She forced her lips to move. "Do you want to play a game with me?"

The reporters realized they were about to witness something juicy, and the cameras began to flash. She ignored them, her entire focus on Galen's expression. Was that hope? Pity? She squashed down her terror and shifted from foot to foot, awaiting his answer.

"What kind of game?" he said finally.

Her pulse clamored, hope sending her heart into overdrive. "I Never."

His guarded eyes went soft and he nodded. "Okay."

She sucked in a deep breath, blocking out the whispers around her to focus solely on Galen. The man she loved.

"I never, in a million years, imagined I could be as happy and fulfilled as I was with you. I never wanted anything more than to spend the rest of my life that way. And if you'll have me, I will never, ever hurt you."

"There you go, girl," Cat whispered.

The room broke out into chatter and Galen stared at her.

"We're discussing a title fight here, young lady. Maybe this isn't the time for—"

"Max is right," Galen cut in. "This is a private issue, Lacey."

She nodded dumbly, tears springing to her eyes. She'd laid it all out there and at least she could say she tried, but that didn't stop the pain. "Sorry." She stumbled down the aisle, Cat hot on her heels whispering apologies when Galen spoke up again.

"No, don't go. That's not what I meant. Everyone *else* can go. Thank you for coming. This press conference is over."

Max bellowed at Galen, and the room exploded. Reporters shoved microphones in her face, shouting questions at her.

"What's your name?"

"How long have you and Galen been together?"

"Are you a fan of boxing?"

Cat stood on a chair and let out a shrill whistle. "All right, listen up, peoples. I'm Galen's sister, Cat, and I'd be happy to tell you the whole sordid tale out in the hallway. It's a goody, featuring a runaway bride and a torrid love affair in paradise. Let's give these two young people some privacy, okay?"

She jumped down and strolled away, leading the pack of reporters like the pied piper. God, Lacey loved that girl. The room cleared, with Max the last to go, shooting her a dirty look. "You better be worth it, chickie."

Soon, it was just Galen and her. She walked around to the side of the table where he sat and looked down at him. All the things she wanted to say, the speech she'd been practicing on the way over, it was all gone. Wiped from her mind like she'd been zapped with one of those *Men in Black* neuralyzers.

"How've you been, squirt?"

Panic lapped at her, and she fumbled for something coherent to say. She was blowing it. Again. "Okay. I quit my job," she blurted.

To his credit, he barely blinked at the oddly timed declaration. "Congratulations."

Now that the cover was off, she couldn't seem to stop. "I'm going back to school. I'm not sure for what yet. I want to find a career I love." The moments ticked by and a band of tension tightened around the back of her neck, like an unseen hand.

"That sounds like a great idea. How did your parents take the news?"

She opened her mouth to give her typical blow-off response and say that she saw things differently than her mother did, and that was okay. But that was a lie. It wasn't okay, and likely never would be. It was time to accept that they would never be close.

"Dad was fine. Mother was Mother. She's not speaking to me right now. Sometimes I think maybe it's for the best. Either way, I'm done trying to placate her. I've done it my whole life, and it's gotten me nowhere. It's not like she loves me more for it or it's helped our relationship in any way. From now on, I'm doing what's right for me."

He pushed his chair back and stood, propping his ass against the table. "And the merger?"

"Dead. Marty seemed so desperate to marry me in spite of what happened that my father got suspicious. He had his people do some digging and found out that the Clemsons were on the SEC's radar and were a few months from an investigation. They had wanted to seal the deal with our firm in hopes of weathering the bad PR over the next year. Once we had that information, my father killed the deal for good. And lo and behold, the sky didn't fall. Everyone still has their jobs, and the board is looking for alternate ways to diversify. It's not the end of the world *or* the end of either business. Marty's family will take a hit to their image, but that's due to some questionable business dealings, not to me."

"You must be relieved."

"I am. And last I heard, Becca and Marty were shopping for rings. I guess when I told him there was no chance of reconciliation, he went back to her."

"How do you feel about that? You angry?"

"Not even a little. I'm still really hurt by what Becca did, but at the same time, if not for her, I'd be Mrs. Clemson right now. I sort of feel like I should buy them some flowers or something."

His lips twisted into a wry smile, and she resisted the urge to reach out and trace them with her forefinger.

She sucked in a breath, a sudden calm overtaking her. "You were wrong. That day, when you said my catching Marty cheating was the best thing that ever happened to me? *You* were the best thing that ever happened to me. Our time in Puerto Rico, loving and talking and boxing. I was never so happy in my life." He opened his mouth to speak but she held up a staying hand. "No, let me say what I came to say."

Taking his hand in hers, she looked deep into his eyes and

spoke from her heart. "It wasn't because we were on vacation or away from the daily grind. And it wasn't because I was hurt, or confused, or on the rebound. It's because I loved you. Hell, I think I've loved you since I was a little girl."

His hand clenched over hers but he didn't speak. She pushed through the fear threatening to choke her and went on. "Remember when you got that poster of Elle MacPherson in the blue bathing suit? I used to daydream of cutting her hair off."

His mouth twitched into a tiny smile. "Are you the one who drew the mustache on her?"

She nodded, her cheeks burning with embarrassment. Who cared about a little humiliation? Galen was smiling at her again and her heart was singing.

"I blamed that on Cat and she never denied it."

"Yeah, well, I'd taken the rap for her so many times before, she figured she owed me one. She couldn't understand my unnatural dislike for the woman."

"I have to admit, that mustache was likely there for a long while before I even noticed. I wasn't looking at her face much." At her long-suffering sigh and muttered, "*Men*," he shrugged. "I was thirteen; what do you want from me?"

"Just for you to share your life with me. That's all."

His leg began to shake, and he nudged her back. For a terrifying second, she thought he might walk away. Instead, he swung her effortlessly into his strong arms.

She squealed in shock and snaked her arms around his neck for support. "Where are we going?"

"To my house and then nowhere. Not for at least a week."

He bent low and pressed his lips to hers. She could feel him trembling and held on tighter, wanting to reassure him that she was there and she wasn't going away. Heat stole through her, melting the cold that had been with her since he'd left Puerto Rico. A long moment later, he tore his mouth away and laid his forehead against hers.

"Ah, Lacey. I can't wait to hold you and feel your body against mine. I don't want you out of my sight until it's sunk in. I love you so much. Walking out of that villa was the hardest thing I ever had to do, but if I hadn't done it, neither of us would have known what we know now." He tucked a stray lock of hair behind her ear. "That this is for real."

"I always knew it was. Please don't doubt that. But my mother—"

"Is a wily one, I know. I had faith that you'd figure it out, but it felt like forever. I was climbing the walls waiting, picking up the phone but then putting it down over and over again. You had to make this decision without me pressuring you. But damn, it took you long enough. I'd almost given up hope. That's the only reason I booked the Hermosa fight. I needed something to focus my energy on if you never came back to me, or I would've gone crazy."

Lacey tucked her head against his chest and groaned. "I wanted to stop you before you even left but I was mixed up. By that point, I was half convinced you were looking for an easy way to break it off. Then when I got home and you didn't call…"

He ran a soothing hand over her back. "It's over now. We're together, and that's all that matters."

"What about your fight and the training? Eight months apart is a long time."

"We don't have to be apart. Do a semester out in Chicago. After the fight, we can decide where we want to live. No matter the outcome, I'm retiring after this match. Now that I'm almost thirty, my body takes longer to bounce back, and I want to walk away healthy. I've been thinking of opening a gym to train young fighters from the inner city, and I can do that almost anywhere as long as there's a city nearby."

A series of clicks caught their attention, and they turned toward the sound at the center of the room. Two reporters who must have escaped Cat's clutches stood, snapping photos without even a hint of remorse.

Galen dropped a kiss on the corner of her mouth. "I don't care if they see. I don't care who knows. I love you." He turned to the reporters and smiled. "You got that, guys? This is the woman I love."

Tears rushed to her eyes, and she sniffled. "You're going to make my mascara run and I'll look awful for the camera."

"I don't care about any of that. Just say you'll come with me."

The pain of the past month evaporated like a puddle in the Sahara as happy emotion clogged her throat, but she forced herself to sound stern. "Only if you promise me one thing."

"What's that, squirt?"

"Never let me go."

He tipped her back and bent forward until his mouth was an inch from hers. "I never will."

Acknowledgments

Thanks to my sister Nicole for teaching me to go for it, balls to the wall, heart first, every time. Even when it's scary.

Thanks to my cp, Riley Murphy, for being so frigging awesome and coming up with the nickname Whalin' Galen.

Thanks to Heather Howland for liking me and my little book, and for all of your input. I think you're the bee's knees.

And last, but not least, thanks to Team Ninja (AKA, my fabulous editor, the incomparable Kerri-Leigh Grady, and my wonderful publicists, Heather Riccio and Sarah Nicolas). You guys all rock. When they say it takes a village, this is what they mean, and I couldn't be happier with my crew.

About the Author

Christine Bell is one half of the happiest couple in the world. She and her handsome hubby currently reside in Pennsylvania with a four-pack of teenage boys and their two dogs, Gimli and Pug. If she gets time off from her duties as maid, chef, chauffeur, or therapist, she can be found reading just about anything she can get her hands on, from Young Adult novels to books on poker theory. She doesn't like root beer, clowns, or bugs (except ladybugs, on account of their cute outfits), but lurves chocolate, going to the movies, the New York Giants, and playing Texas Hold 'Em. Writing is her passion, but if she had to pick another occupation, she would be a pirate…or, like, a ninja maybe. She loves writing fun and adventure-filled romance stories, but also hopes to one day publish something her dad can read without wanting to dig his eyes out with rusty spoons.

Christine loves to hear from her readers and can be contacted through her website, www.christine-bell.com or on Twitter under the handle @_ChristineBell

Unleash your inner vixen with these sexy bestselling Brazen releases...

Wrong Bed, Right Guy by **Katee Robert**
Prim and proper art gallery coordinator Elle Walser is no good at seducing men. She slips into her boss's bed in the hopes of winning his heart, but instead, finds herself in the arms of Gabe Schultz, his bad boy nightclub mogul brother. Has Elle's botched seduction led her to the right bed after all?

Seducing Cinderella by **Gina L. Maxwell**
Mixed martial arts fighter Reid Andrews needs to reclaim his title. Lucie Miller needs seduction lessons to catch the eye of another man. They agree to help each other, but by the end of their respective trainings, Reid and Lucy might just discover they've already found what they desire most...

No Flowers Required by **Cari Quinn**
A night of passion is all down-on-her-luck flower shop owner Alexa Conroy wants, but when she propositions a sexy stranger, she gets more than she bargained for. Dillon James isn't who he says he is. Will saving her company be enough to protect their love from Dillon's lies?

Her Forbidden Hero by **Laura Kaye**
Former Army Special Forces Sgt. Marco Vieri has never thought of Alyssa Scott as more than his best friend's little sister, but her return home changes that. Now that she's back in his life, will he become her forbidden hero, and can she heal him, one touch at a time?

One Night with a Hero by **Laura Kaye**

After growing up with an abusive, alcoholic father, Army Special Forces Sgt. Brady Scott vowed never to have a family of his own. But when a hot one-night stand with new neighbor Joss Daniels leads to an unexpected pregnancy, can he let go of his past and create a new future with her?

Tempting the Best Man by **J. Lynn**

Madison Daniels has worshipped her brother's best friend since they were kids, but they've blurred the lines before and now they can't stop bickering. Forced together for her brother's wedding getaway, will they call a truce or strangle each other first?

Tempting the Player by **J. Lynn**

After the paparazzi catches him in a compromising position, baseball bad boy Chad Gamble is issued an ultimatum: fake falling in love with the feisty redhead in the pictures, or kiss his multi-million dollar contract goodbye. Too bad being blackmailed into a relationship with Chad is the last thing Bridget Rodgers needs.

Recipe for Satisfaction by **Gina Gordon**

Famous bad boy restaurateur Jack Vaughn is trying to find his way back to the living when he meets the beautiful Sterling Andrews, a professional organizer hell-bent on seducing the tattooed hottie as part of her fresh take on life. Too bad she's Jack's newest employee, and totally off-limits.

Made in the USA
Middletown, DE
28 April 2018